HARLEQ Prese

Fantastic Stories for Fall!

Emma Darcy is back with *The Playboy Boss's Chosen Bride*, the story of arrogant Jake Devila and Merlina, who grabs her chance to make him see that she's not just his dowdy, reliable secretary. Penny Jordan is on sizzling form with *Master of Pleasure*: Sasha thought she'd walked away from Gabriel Cabrini, but now he possesses her once more. Julia James guarantees dark desire in *Purchased for Revenge*: Greek tycoon Alexei Constantin has only one thing on his mind—vengeance. If that means bedding Eve he'll do it. Jane Porter delivers drama, glamour and intense emotion when Spanish superstar Wolf Kerrick claims Alexandra, his rags-to-riches bride, in *Hollywood Husband, Contract Wife*. For a touch of regal romance, choose *The Rich Man's Royal Mistress*, the second part of Robyn Donald's trilogy, THE ROYAL HOUSE OF ILLYRIA. Virginal Princess Melissa falls under the spell of man-of-the-world billionaire Hawke Kennedy. In Elizabeth Power's compelling *The Millionaire's Love-Child*, Annie and former boss, Brant Cadman, are reunited in a marriage of convenience when they discover that their babies were swapped at birth. While Anton, the Comte de Valois, demands that Diana become his bride when she becomes pregnant. But what is behind his proposal? Find out in *The French Count's Pregnant Bride* by Catherine Spencer. Bought and bedded by the sheikh—the explosive passion between Prince Malik and Abbie could turn an arranged marriage into one of Eastern delight in Kate Walker's *At the Sheikh's Command*.

Julia James

PURCHASED FOR REVENGE

Bedded by...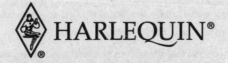

Forced to bed...then to wed?

HARLEQUIN®

TORONTO • NEW YORK • LONDON
AMSTERDAM • PARIS • SYDNEY • HAMBURG
STOCKHOLM • ATHENS • TOKYO • MILAN • MADRID
PRAGUE • WARSAW • BUDAPEST • AUCKLAND

ISBN-13: 978-0-373-12573-9
ISBN-10:   0-373-12573-9

PURCHASED FOR REVENGE

First North American Publication 2006.

All about the author…
Julia James

JULIA JAMES lives in England with her family. Harlequin® novels were the first "grown-up" books she read as a teenager, alongside Georgette Heyer and Daphne du Maurier, and she's been reading them ever since. Julia adores the British countryside—in all its seasons, and is fascinated by all things historical, from castles to cottages. She also has a special love for the Mediterranean—"the most perfect landscape after England!"—and considers both ideal settings for romance stories! Since becoming a romance writer, she has, she says, had the great good fortune to start discovering the Caribbean, as well, and is happy to report that those magical, beautiful islands are also ideal settings for romance stories. "One of the best things about writing romance is that it gives you a great excuse to take holidays in fabulous places," says Julia. "All in the name of research, of course!"

Her first stab at novel writing was Regency romances. "But, alas, no one wanted to publish them," she says. She put her writing aside until her family commitments were clear, and then renewed her love affair with contemporary romances. "My writing partner and I made a pact not to give up until we were published—and we both succeeded! Natasha Oakley writes for Mills & Boon® Tender Romance™, and we faithfully read each other's works in progress and give each other a lot of free advice and encouragement."

In between writing Julia enjoys walking, gardening, needlework, baking "extremely gooey chocolate cakes"—and trying to stay fit!

PROLOGUE

ALEXEI CONSTANTIN slid into the dark leather seat of the large, sleek black car waiting for him at the kerb, the door having been opened promptly for him by the uniformed chauffeur. The door closed, the chauffeur took his place at the wheel, started the engine and moved off into the early morning London traffic.

For a brief moment Alexei contemplated how easily he took such luxurious comfort for granted now, how easily he accepted the vast distance he'd travelled in the fifteen years since he'd set out for the Adriatic ferry port on his eighteenth birthday, a scrawny teenager with little more than the clothes he was wearing, and with his dark eyes burning.

Now, the same dark eyes no longer burned. They were veiled. Unreadable.

Long lashes swept down over high cheekbones as he settled his lean shoulders against the smooth leather upholstery and picked up the topmost of the sheaf of newspapers that had been placed on the seat beside him, extracting the company news section. He glanced at the distinctive pink newsprint of the *Financial Times*.

'*Hawkwood—AC International tightens the net*' announced the headline.

He read the article swiftly, scanning the lines, his face expressionless. With the same methodical swiftness he worked his way through the papers. Only one caused him to pause.

It was a photograph, clearly taken at some society event, sited beside yet another news story about AC International's takeover battle for Hawkwood Enterprises. Alexei's gaze stilled as he looked down at the image in front of him.

Giles Hawkwood.

The man dominated the photograph, the way he sought to dominate anything and everything. He was wearing evening dress, the tuxedo straining across his thickening torso. His familiar features, with the characteristic strong nose, were framed by thick greying hair. He was looking his age, thought Alexei, his regard emotionless. For a moment he did nothing except look at the face of the man who was the object of the remorseless siege that he was conducting. Then, having taken his fill, he allowed his gaze to take in his companions.

There were two women, one either side of Hawkwood. One was of the same generation, although her handsome features were immaculately preserved. The Honourable Amabel Hawkwood, daughter of the sixth Viscount Duncaster, looked out at the world with a haughty, patrician expression. Acidly, Alexei wondered whether she looked so haughty and patrician at the extremely discreet detox clinic she was rumoured to habitually frequent.

His eyes slid to the other woman, standing on Hawkwood's left.

She was facing away from the camera, turned towards someone else cropped out of the photo.

His eyes narrowed, his gaze arrested.

There was little to see of her beyond a bare shoulder, the line of her evening gown and the pale fall of her hair, a glint of diamond at the lobe of her ear. But Alexei knew who she was.

Eve Hawkwood, twenty-five years old and only child of Giles Hawkwood.

He felt his mouth tug into a cynical twist.

Like her aristocratic mother, Eve Hawkwood was a sophisticated socialite, adorning her wealthy father's arm at glittering events such as the one where this photo had been taken. With her father's money backing her, Eve Hawkwood could spend her life swanning around the luxurious places of the world, buying all the clothes she wanted, indulging herself all day long.

She had no need for anything as menial as a job.

Alexei's expression grew even more cynical. Except that Eve Hawkwood, it was rumoured, did in fact work for a living.

If you could call it work.

Giles Hawkwood, a man who got what he wanted by any means he considered effective, was not averse, so the rumours ran, to exploiting all the resources he had to hand. Not only had he married the Honourable Amabel for her social standing, putting up with her well-known little 'weakness' which kept her increasingly out of circulation, but he was also not averse to making the most of his daughter's youth and beauty.

Alexei stared down at the photo. He might not be able to make out Eve Hawkwood's features, but there was a tilt to her averted chin, a straightness to her spine, that gave her an air echoing her mother's—a hauteur, a remoteness, an untouchability in every line of her body.

Again Alexei's mouth twisted. Except Eve Hawkwood, so he had heard, was not untouchable at all.

But only—his dark eyes hardened—only when Daddy told her not to be…

Abruptly, he tossed the newspaper aside.

Neither Eve Hawkwood nor the Honourable Amabel were of the slightest interest to him. They were not in his sights at all. Only Giles Hawkwood.

His prey.

CHAPTER ONE

EVE sat in the wide, soft leather aeroplane seat, legs slanted gracefully to one side, flicking unseeingly through a copy of *Vogue*. There was only one other passenger in the private jet winging its way south over France towards the Côte d'Azur. Across the aisle her father was working through papers, a frown on his face, his jaw clamped tight.

His mood was grim, Eve knew. It had been growing grimmer ever since the takeover bid by AC International had been launched. At first her father had been contemptuous, sneering, but as one shareholder after another had started to look favourably on the bid, or succumb to the lure of the premium price AC International was offering for Hawkwood shares, his reaction had changed.

The takeover bid had become a battle. A battle her father was now taking to the man who had the audacity to try and wrest his company from him.

'When I come face to face with him it's got to look like nothing more than a coincidence,' he'd barked at Eve. 'If you're with me it will just look like a social occasion.'

It was a familiar role for Eve to be required to play. The socially poised daughter, the charming guest, the gracious hostess—whenever her father required youthful but respectable female company. Eve's eyes hardened. The times when far from respectable females had been at her father's side were plentiful. She could still remember the shock and disgust she'd felt when she'd turned up unexpectedly at her father's Mayfair apartment once, as a student, to find a party in full swing. Except the word 'party' didn't even begin to describe it.

Naked and half-naked girls had lolled about the apartment, many of whom clearly there for the purpose of 'sexual entertainment'—if that was the polite term for what was going on—and a blue movie flickering in the background on a huge plasma screen.

Since then she'd had no illusions about what her father did to amuse himself when he wasn't increasing his wealth and being a complete s.o.b. to everyone around him. And he certainly wasn't the only one to amuse himself that way.

A look of repugnance shadowed her eyes. And foreboding.

When it came to that kind of partying some of the worst rich men were the newest rich men—especially those who came from countries just discovering how to make serious money.

Would this Alexei Constantin be like that? The country he came from was one of those in South Eastern Europe that seemed to have sprung up overnight in the last fifteen years after the fall of communism. What she knew of the place—Dalaczia—was minimal, though she'd looked it up a bit since last night. It would, she assumed hopefully, be a safe topic of conversation if she had to find one with the man. So far she had learned that Dalaczia shared a border with Greece, possessed a short Adriatic seaboard and some offshore islands, was mostly mountainous, and had been fought over for centuries by every power in the region, including Russia, Turkey, Austria, Greece, Italy and assorted Balkan states. The official religion was Orthodox, and the alphabet was a variation on Cyrillic. Its present independence was precarious and unstable—so was its current government. Not that Eve intended to discuss either—that could swiftly become contentious. Instead she had a list of notable natural features, some data on flora and fauna, and a smidgen of folk customs. That would have to do.

As for the man himself—well, if she was to go by the stereotype currently so popular in American films, Alexei Constantin would doubtless be some florid, overweight, middle-aged man, with a fleshy face and gold teeth, who'd made a bundle out of ruthlessly expropriating his country's assets since the fall of communism.

She gave a suppressed sigh. So what if he was? Her only task would be to make polite conversation with him until her father decided it was time to despatch her to her quarters and talk business. Her father's gloves would come off then. He fought rough, and very, very dirty—who knew better than she? Eve thought bitterly. But whatever he had planned for Alexei Constantin, she didn't want to know.

She didn't want to know anything of what her father did. She just wanted to keep him away from her life as much as she could. Not that that was easy, or even possible. Giles Hawkwood cast a long shadow.

She'd lived under it all her life.

And there was, she knew, no escape.

No escape at all.

Her reflection gazed back at her from the mirror of the vanity unit in the lavish ladies' room on the ground floor of the Riviera hotel, and Eve studied it. It was the way she liked to look. Silvery-grey Grecian style evening gown with a draped bodice, pale hair in a coiled chignon, simple drop pearl earrings and matching necklace, subtle make up and hint of classic fragrance.

She looked cool, detached. Untroubled by the worries of the world. Cocooned and sheltered, the pampered daughter of one of the UK's richest men, with a flat in Chelsea and charge cards for every designer store in London.

That was what the outside world saw.

Only she knew different.

For a moment, her eyes shadowed.

Then, lifting her chin, she got to her feet. She had a role to play and no choice in the casting, and that was that.

She walked across the hotel's lobby, and paused at the entrance to the casino, her eyes quickly locating the table where her father was sitting, cognac glass at his elbow, wreathed in cigar fumes. Steeling herself, she straightened her spine and prepared to head back to her post at his side, as she was supposed to do.

Out of nowhere, a wave of depression hit her, crushing her with its weight. She'd lived like this so *long*—all her adult life—jerked on a string by her father, summoned when he wanted her for something, dismissed when he'd done with her, doing his bidding whenever it suited him.

If only I could escape—not be his daughter...be someone totally, completely different.

For a moment the desire was so intense she couldn't breathe. Then, with a jolt, her lungs opened to take in air again.

And she stilled.

There was a man walking from the bar area at the far side of the casino towards the wide arched doorway where she was standing. He was walking with a lithe, but purposeful gait, threading his way between the tables. For one totally absurd, irrational moment, Eve thought he was walking towards her. For an even briefer moment she felt her mouth suddenly dry. Then she realised he was simply heading for the lobby, and would need to pass her to do so.

Automatically she made to move her gaze away from him.

But she couldn't.

Helplessly, she found herself watching him, unable to look away. Her mouth went dry again.

He was slimly built, his tuxedo fitting like a smooth glove over his svelte figure. She was used to seeing men in bespoke evening dress, but very few of them ever filled them as well as this man did.

But then, she acknowledged, very few of them had physiques remotely comparable to this man's.

Or, she realised, with a strange, breathless hollowing of her stomach, the looks to go with the physique. Dark hair, cut short, narrow face, high cheekbones, a blade of a nose and eyes—eyes that seemed as dark as a deep mountain lake caught in a hollow where the sunlight seldom reaches.

Something jolted through her, sucking the breath from her. She wanted to look—to keep looking. Her mind was racing almost as fast as her heart-rate.

He wasn't English; that was certain. Nor French nor Italian. Not Mediterranean, perhaps. So what, then? She frowned very slightly. The high cheekbones seemed almost Slavic, yet his skin tone was Mediterranean—or close by.

Whatever his racial origins, one fact about him was indisputable—he was the most arresting male she had ever set eyes on.

She could not pull her eyes away.

But she must.

She must because it did not *matter* that he was the most arresting male she'd ever seen. There was absolutely no point in thinking him so. No point in standing here gazing at him like some gawky teenager. No point feeling this sudden dryness of her mouth, the breathlessness in her lungs, the senseless racing of her heart-rate. No point at all.

She wasn't here to go stupid over a man. Any man.

She *never* went stupid over a man. Not since she'd realised, after she'd left school and started to look out at the adult world, that being Eve Hawkwood was not exactly an advantage when it came to romance. Whatever beauty she possessed, very few men ever saw past the looming presence of Giles Hawkwood.

She certainly could not, she knew bitterly.

And tonight—here—of all times and places—her father's shadow was darkening everything.

So there was only one thing to be done. Look away. Tear her eyes away from the man walking towards where she stood and let him walk by. Take no further notice of him—because, after all, what would be the point of doing otherwise?

No point, she knew.

With a huge effort, more than she'd thought she would have to make, she tried to tear her eyes away.

It was too late.

Out of nowhere, suddenly, as he strode past the last of the *vingt-et-un* tables, the man's eyes flicked to hers.

And the breath was crushed from her lungs.

It was like a blow impacting. But not with pain.

With something quite different.

Almost, Alexei paused in his stride. But not quite. It didn't stop his eyes fastening to hers, though. Didn't stop the sudden instinctive tightening that he felt.

She was blonde. Incredibly blonde. Pale hair and pale skin. With the fine-boned looks that only the English possessed.

And she was stunning with it. Perfect wide-set grey eyes, a slender nose, and a mouth that was slightly, *very* slightly parted.

Her body was tall, graceful, and perfectly proportioned. Long legs, rounded hips, hand-span waist and two perfect orbs for breasts. All covered by a silver-grey evening dress that was as subtly understated as her extraordinary beauty was not.

He felt the tightening again.

Hell, this was not the moment for this to happen—

He didn't need this. Not now. Not here. Not when all his energies had to be focussed on the one thing he was so close, *so* close, to achieving. The thing that had driven him, possessed him, all his adult life.

I haven't got time for this...

The hard, pitiless knowledge slammed through him.

He had to stop this. Now.

It was too late. His eyes had locked on to hers.

It lasted only a few seconds, but it was enough. Enough to send a shockwave through him that he could feel resonating in every cell in his body.

Desire bit through him.

And something else. Something he was not used to feeling. Something he could not identify.

For a handful of seconds his eyes held hers, as the distance between them shortened. She stood absolutely immobile, doing nothing, nothing at all, except locking her eyes to his. As if that was all that was keeping her upright.

He felt his stride slowing, preparing to stop, to pause. To veer towards her...

No! He hadn't got time for this—this was the wrong time, the wrong place.

But the right woman?

The voice whispered in his head. He silenced it. Ruthlessly he slammed it down with all the rigid self-control he steered his life by. He swept his lashes down over his eyes to shut her from his sight.

As the lashes swept upwards again he realised that she had gone.

Eve bolted. Slipping sideways, she twisted away and hurried as fast as her high heels would let her towards the plate glass doors that led out towards the pool deck overlooking the sea. Her heart was beating like a wild thing, and her cheeks were suddenly burning.

Oh, dear heaven—

Her mind was in chaos. She felt as if a jolt of electricity had just been blasted through her body without warning.

Those eyes, looking straight into hers...

Heat fanned through her again. She took a tumbling breath

and kept walking as rapidly as she could, not paying the slightest attention to where she was going.

Nothing like this had ever happened to her before! Where on earth had it come from? What was it about that man that had overset her like this? She sucked air into her stomach and tried to steady her breathing, deliberately slowing her hectic pace.

As she did, determinedly calming her breath, even if there was nothing she could do for her racing heart-rate, she tried to get a grip of herself.

You just saw a fantastic-looking male. That was all. You've seen a lot of them in your time. They're not exactly uncommon in the world.

Even as she reasoned with herself, she knew what she said was not true. There might be fantastic-looking males in the world, and she might have seen a lot of them—but none had ever made her react like that to them. None had made her just want to stare, and stare, and stare at them, while her heart-rate went crazy inside her and her breathing stopped.

His image leapt into her mind's eye. She could recall it perfectly, and even just recalling it sent a frisson through her.

Something about him…

Again she felt that frisson go through her, as she remembered the endless moment when his eyes had locked to hers, jolting electricity through her with a voltage she'd never experienced before.

His eyes had done something to her that she couldn't explain. It wasn't lust. God knew she'd been on the receiving end of looks like that ever since she was a teenager. This was something much, much more powerful. Much more disturbing.

Much more devastating.

Her heart-rate started to clatter again, and she felt her pace increase. This time she let it. She'd realised where she was now. On a paved terrace that led along the rocky edge of the sea between the hotel's gardens and the Mediterranean. The path led through pine trees, which blessedly shielded the lights from the hotel, and ended, she knew from previous visits to the hotel—one of her father's favourites, thanks both to the casino and the marina where he had his yacht moored—at a miniature promontory overlooking the sea, set with stone seats from which to look at the view in daytime.

She gained it within a few more minutes, but did not sit down. The stone would be too cold with nothing to protect her but her thin evening dress. Instead she leant against the balustrade, trying to steady her breath, her pulse, and gazed out over the night-darkened Mediterranean, at the tiny waves breaking on the rocks below the terrace. Above her, stars were pricking out, and behind her the moon was starting to rise. An almost imperceptible breeze came off the sea, tugging her hair into tendrils around her face, freeing them from the confines of the low chignon at the nape of her neck. The mild night air netted her, the scent of the sea and the pines quieted her. Slowly she felt the heat seep from her cheeks, her heart-rate slow.

And into its place came a yearning that was almost a sadness.

What did it matter that she'd just set eyes on a man who had had such an extraordinary effect on her? It was pointless thinking about him. Quite pointless. She was unlikely to see him again, as he had clearly been heading out of the casino, and very probably the hotel, but even if he weren't, so what? Nothing whatsoever could possibly come of her reacting to him like that.

Nothing.

All he could ever be was a fantasy. No one real. No one who could possibly have anything to do with her. Just a vague dream of what might have been in a different life.

That was all. Nothing more than that.

She went on looking out over the dark sea, her eyes as shadowed as the night.

* * *

She should not have run. That had been a mistake.

Alexei watched for a fraction of a second as she hurried across the hotel lobby to the rear doors facing the sea.

If she'd simply gone on standing there as he'd walked past her he'd have let her be. There was every reason to let her be. None at all for what he was now doing—striding after her with long, lean steps. Deliberately he did not catch up with her. Deliberately he let her reach the outdoors and plunge off to the left of the hotel. He didn't know where she was going, but he would find out.

The area she was heading into was far less brightly lit than the deck immediately behind the hotel. Only the occasional low-level light marked the pathway she was hurrying along. He watched her for a moment, watched as her speed gradually slowed and she gained a stand of pine trees, then was lost to view in the dim light.

Alexei's eyes glinted.

At a relaxed, leisurely pace, he set off after her.

He knew he shouldn't. He knew it was the wrong time and the wrong place.

But she was definitely the right woman.

The most right woman he'd ever seen.

He'd only seen her for an instant, but he'd never, ever had such a kick to his system from any woman before—and he was not, *not* prepared to let her walk out of his life before he'd even walked into it. He was being rash, he was being reckless, he was being stupid—he knew that all too well. But he knew what he wanted right now.

He wanted to find her.

It was the footsteps she heard first. With instinctive alarm, Eve whipped her head round at the sound of someone approaching. The hotel and grounds were private, and with so many wealthy people here security was high, if unobtrusive. But she was at the far end of the gardens, a place no one was likely to be at this time of night. So who on earth was—?

As he stepped out of the deep shadow of the pine trees her breath caught, and held. For a moment she thought it could not be real. That she'd simply conjured the tall, lean figure out of the air, out of her memory. But the man walking towards her now wasn't a fantasy.

He was very, very real.

'You shouldn't have run,' he said.

He spoke French. There was an underlying accent, she could tell, but she couldn't identify what his native language might be. The part of her brain that was capable of any kind of rational thought was not functioning.

She gazed at him helplessly as he walked towards her. Her heart had started to beat. Not racing, but with slow, heavy beats that seemed to take an eternity. Time seemed to be slowing down around her.

He came up to her.

She could not see his face properly in the dim light. The moonlight slanted across his face, turning it to planes and shadows. Turning her limbs to sponge. Her hands tightened on the stone balustrade. She ignored the cold that bit into her flesh.

It was the only part of her that was cold. In the rest of her a slow heat was burning.

'Why did you? Run?'

The sound of his voice, with its low-pitched, accented timbre, caught at her senses.

'I don't know.'

It sounded to her ears such a stupid answer to make. But it was an honest one. It drew a slight smile from him. An indentation of his mouth. Her eyes went to it, drawn irresistibly. It did something to her. Something that fanned the slow-burning heat inside her and sucked the breath out of her lungs. She felt herself stepping back from the balustrade, letting go of it. Her arms fell helplessly to her sides.

What was happening? What was happening here, now, with this man who had drawn her eyes like a magnet as he'd approached her, and from whom she had run, fled, sensing an imperative that she must if she had any sanity obey, because he was only a fantasy, *could* only be a fantasy, nothing more? And yet he had come after her, followed her here, now…and she did not know why…

. 'I just knew that I had to run…'

Her voice was still low, strange even to her ears.

He took another step towards her.

'You don't have to run from me,' he said.

Eve looked at him. The shadowed light was still etching his face, the moonlight glinting off his eyes. There was something in his eyes…

He murmured something. She did not understand it. It was not French, or English. There had only been a few words, and she could not identify the language. Then he was speaking again, this time in English.

'Who are you?'

Expression flickered in her face. Her lips parted, but she did not speak. She did not want to speak. Did not want to tell him who she was. It didn't matter whether this man had or hadn't heard of her father—and anyway, why should he have? There were a lot of rich people in the world and they did not all know each other. It was because suddenly, urgently, she wanted to be…someone quite different. A woman who could, if she wanted, walk out under the Mediterranean sky and gaze into the eyes of a fantasy come to life…

Prevarication came to her.

'Why do you think I'm English?' she answered, sticking to French.

The smile indented at his mouth again, and yet again she felt her breath catch.

'Aren't you?' he mocked, very gently, keeping to English.

His words, accented as they were, with that strange, elusive accent, resonated through her. She gave a tiny shrug of her shoulders.

'You're not French either,' she returned, still in that language.

'No,' he agreed, but said no more.

Eve knew why. Like her, he did not want this moment to be encumbered by nationalities, identities, categories and classifications. Like her, he wanted it to be—pure. That was the word that formed in her mind. *Pure.*

Out here, in the clean, fresh air, with the wind from the sea soughing so gently in the tall pine trees, in the clear moonlit night, it was nothing to do with the luxury world of the hotel, with its high-stakes casino, its three-star Michelin restaurant, its marina for multimillion-pound yachts, and its car park full of deluxe cars for deluxe people.

Nothing to do with the world of her father. Beyond the reach of his long, malign shadow.

She knew she was being foolish. She couldn't escape from being who she was, what she was. Nor could this man here, who might possibly be some kind of impostor, interloper, but who was, she knew, with the deep recognition and experience of the world she had been brought up in, one of the rich men of the world.

But for this short space of time they would both escape from who they were, what they were.

'Why did you follow me here?' She spoke in French still. She didn't quite know why.

He smiled again, not a mere indentation of his mouth, but almost a laugh, lifting his face, showing the whiteness of his teeth.

'No Frenchwoman would ask that!' The mockery was there again, but it was conspiratorial, not cruel.

She gave an answering, unwilling smile, acknowledging her mistake.

'And no woman,' he went on—and his voice had changed, the timbre deepening, sending the heat seeping through her veins again, 'as beautiful as you need ask that question.'

For a moment he held her eyes, then hers flickered away, uncertain. As they did so the breeze freshened over her bare arms, and she gave a slight shiver.

He was there immediately. He stripped off his tuxedo jacket and draped it around her shoulders. The warmth from his body was still in the silk lining. Eve felt her throat tighten. It was so intimate a gesture. She felt her heart-rate flutter again.

His hands were still on her shoulders as he stood half behind her. She twisted her head back.

'Thank you.' Her voice was low, almost breathless.

His face was close. Far too close. Far, far too close. The world disappeared. Simply ceased to exist. Only his eyes existed, looking deep into hers. Moonlight reflected in their depths. A pulse beat at her throat. She felt her hand move, reach up, and with the lightest touch her fingers traced his jaw. She felt it tense beneath her feathering touch. Saw the pupils of his eyes flare. Heard the intake of breath in his throat. Caught the heady, masculine scent of him.

Then her hand fluttered free, and her mouth dried at what she had just done. Touched a complete stranger like that. Instinctively, impulsively, she pulled away, stepping forward to seize the balustrade again.

'I'm sorry!' The apology rushed from her in a low, abashed voice. Her head lowered, and she gazed unseeingly down at the wavelets lapping on the rocks below the terrace. She bit her lip.

'You apologise?' She could hear his accent. It shivered down her spine, rippling through her blood. Setting her body resonating finely, so finely…

He had stepped close to her again, was standing behind her now. And once again she felt the pressure of his hands on her shoulders, through the fine material of the jacket he'd draped around her. The pressure seemed to anchor her to the earth, the turning earth.

'There is no need to apologise.' She could hear amusement in his voice, but something else ran beneath the amusement.

He turned her around. Her back was against the balustrade, and he was standing right in front of her. His hands slipped to either side of her face, long, strong fingers sliding into her hair. He was tall, taller than her, looking down at her. His hair was sable in the night.

She gazed at him. Helpless. Motionless.

She did not breathe. Did not do anything, anything at all, that might break this moment. Might shatter the reality of what was happening. She was standing here, in the moonlight, by the sea's edge, and this man, whom she did not know, could never know, held her face in his hands and looked down at her.

He kissed her.

She saw his head start to lower, realised in that fraction of a second what he was going to do. Realised, in that same fraction of a second, that she would let him. That she would rather die than not let this man kiss her here, now, like this, in this moment out of time, out of reality. Out of sanity.

She closed her eyes.

Closed her eyes and let him kiss her. A stranger whom she would never know, whom she *could* never know. A stranger she would walk away from. She would never have this moment again.

But she would have it now. Just for these few, precious seconds. An eye-blink in time.

But hers now. Here.

And nothing, no one, could take it away from her.

Her lips parted.

He kissed her slowly, like honey, grazing her with a velvet touch, moving over her mouth like softest silk.

Then his head lifted away, his hands dropped from her face.

She opened her eyes.

His face was different somehow, his eyes different.

And at that moment something tremored through her. The world went still again. So still.

Then, into the stillness and the silence, she heard the sound of a motor boat intrude, coming out of the marina on the far side of the hotel and heading out to sea, towards one of the rings of lights that marked the presence of a motor yacht moored in deep water.

Her eyes flared. Reality flooded back. The world started up again.

'I have to go!'

She slipped out from where she was, undraping the tuxedo jacket as she did so, and thrusting it towards him.

'Wait—'

It was a command. She obeyed. Her breath was tight in her chest.

'I have to go,' she repeated.

Her hand lifted, almost as if to reach to touch his sleeve, so short a distance away. Then, her eyes flaring again, she whirled around, gathered her skirts, and ran.

Like Cinderella from her ball.

But leaving behind no glass slipper.

Alexei watched her go. This time he let her run. He didn't want to. He wanted to stride after her and seize her back. Stop her running. Keep her.

Hold her.

Fold his arms around her and hold her very close.

Instead, he let her go. He had no choice, he knew.

Reality had flooded back. The reality of what his life was about.

And what it was about was *not* this. Not holding in his arms a woman who had taken his breath away, who had been, for these few brief, fleeting moments, like a sip of purest spring water after stagnant dregs. Whose lips had touched his and in that touch touched more. Touched something deep inside…

No. Grimly he shrugged on his tuxedo jacket again. This was just some fantasy he could not afford. Not now.

Reality was waiting for him. Waiting for him as it had waited all his life. Hard and unyielding. And there was no escape from it.

He headed back to the hotel.

CHAPTER TWO

EVE walked back into the casino. The heat, the constant murmur, the smell of wine and cognac, the fumes of cigars and cigarettes, the heavy perfumes and scented air, oppressed her instantly. But she ignored it. Steadily, she threaded her way towards her father. The pile of chips at his side had diminished. So had the level of cognac in his glass. There was the stub of a cigar in the ashtray, and another was between his thick fingers as he pushed more chips onto a square.

Silently, she took her place behind him. He acknowledged her resumed presence only by a low, perfunctory admonition.

'You took your time.'

'I needed some fresh air,' she said. Her voice was very calm, her manner composed. After all, what else was there for her to be? What else was there to do but what she had been brought here to do, to be a social foil for her father?

Who else was there for her to be except her father's daughter? Eve Hawkwood.

She wasn't anyone else. She wasn't a woman who could weave dreams about a man she had seen for no more than a few minutes walking towards her, who'd made her body still, her heart race, her breath stop. She wasn't a woman who could kiss that same stranger in the moonlight. It was a fantasy, nothing more, conjured by her own longing for escape.

For a second, piercing and anguished, she felt again what she had felt as she had lifted her mouth to his, felt again the cool slide of his hands to cup her face, long fingers grazing in her hair, felt again her eyes start to shut…

No. Rigidly she held them open again. Made them look, with her habitual composure, her inexpressive indifference, at the scene in front of her, at the spinning whirl of the roulette wheel, the chips conducting their remorseless dance around the table, from player to chequered cloth, to croupier to player. Hypnotic in its remorselessness.

Then, with an awareness of her father's mood that her instinct for survival and self-preservation had honed since childhood, she saw his shoulders tense.

She looked up from the table.

Blackness drummed in on her. Her hand groped automatically for the back of her father's chair. Vision blurred, then cleared.

The man she had just kissed was walking towards the roulette table.

For one blazing, incandescent moment, Eve's heart leapt. Then, like a slow draining, she realised that he was not looking at her.

Not looking *for* her.

And even as she realised that, she realised too that somewhere, buried deep inside, there had been a hope—frail, pathetic, but there all the same—that the man who had turned her limbs to water with a single glance from his dark, compelling eyes would not let her run from him. Would not let that single, momentary kiss be enough. The slow draining of that frail pathetic hope was complete.

He had not even seen her. Had not even registered her presence.

She was invisible to him.

He had kissed her so short a time ago, but now he did not know her. Did not see her.

But even as she let go of the last remnant of her futile hope, leaving a dry, drained emptiness inside her, she realised why he was not looking at her.

And as she did, a dark, ominous foreboding began to gel inside her.

He was not walking towards the roulette table. He was walking towards her father.

And something about the way he was walking sent a chill down her spine.

Controlled. Purposeful.

Deadly.

The word formed in her mind, and she could not unform it. It hung there, making her stomach pool with cold.

She tensed in every muscle.

Hawkwood had paused in his play. Alexei saw his hand still a moment, before continuing to position the next batch of chips he was pointlessly sacrificing to his own arrogant bluff—the bluff that said he could afford to lose, and go on losing, the way he was tonight.

Alexei knew better. Giles Hawkwood could not afford to lose a penny more. His yacht, his properties, every possible asset, had all been securitised to raise cash to buy up his own company shares wherever he could find them. But he was too late. As of this morning, AC International had agreed to acquire—in a very friendly and mutually profitable merger—an Australian company that just happened to possess a sufficient number of Hawkwood shares to give Alexei the undisputed majority holding.

Giles Hawkwood was—finally—in the palm of his hand.

Powerless, and broke.

He just didn't know it yet.

And Alexei didn't have any intention of letting him know it yet.

He wanted to savour the knowledge that he would be meeting

his prey for the first—and last—time, and his prey did not even know that he was beaten.

He reached the roulette table, and stopped.

Waiting. Waiting for Giles Hawkwood to make his move.

'Constantin.'

Eve heard her father say the name, but his reason for saying it did not register. All that registered was that the man whom she had thought a fantasy, whom she had kissed in the moonlight, by the sea's edge, from whom she had run because there was nothing else for her to do, was now standing a handful of metres away from her, on the other side of the roulette table. The people sitting there had automatically, it seemed, made way for him, and now he stood looking across and down at her father.

For a moment he said nothing, yet Eve felt her stomach pool with cold again.

Then, with a slow welling of disbelief, the name her father had addressed him by registered.

Constantin.

Alexei Constantin.

This was Alexei Constantin.

Shock knifed through her. And hollowing disbelief. She felt herself sway, and grip the chair-back as if it alone kept her upright.

Then her father leant back. Instinctively, automatically, she pulled her hand away.

She never touched her father. Never let him touch her.

He was looking across at Alexei Constantin, who was looking back down at him. His face was unreadable, expressionless. But there was something in it, in the controlled stance of his body, that was completely, absolutely different from the man who had walked towards her on the terrace such a short time ago.

This was a different man.

Her father took a deep inhalation from his cigar, then rested it against the ashtray. His eyes never left the other man's.

'So,' he said, 'an opportune encounter, wouldn't you say?'

His voice was grating.

Even, to Eve's ears, baiting.

Alexei Constantin's expression did not change. 'Would I?' he responded.

His voice was different. As different as the man who looked down at her father with that chill, expressionless face.

She realised, with a start of unease, that the play at the roulette table had halted. So had the conversation around the table. Everyone was focussing on the exchange taking place.

It must be obvious to her father as well. His eyes moved dismissively, then he nodded at Alexei Constantin.

'Come to dinner tomorrow night. On my yacht.' He lifted his cigar again, and took another leisurely puff from his cigar, relaxing more deeply into the chair carrying his bulk. 'I'll send the launch at, oh, say half-eight?'

His eyes, pouched from burgundy and cognac, were heavy.

For the briefest moment Alexei Constantin did not speak. Then he gave the very slightest nod.

'Make it nine. I like to check the Asia Pacific opening prices. It's always interesting to see what's moved.'

Now it was his turn for his voice to be baiting. Eve saw the colour mount fleetingly in her father's mottled cheeks, then subside again.

'You do that,' he contented himself with responding. Then, as if to regain the upper hand, he snapped his fingers at the croupier to resume play, and pushed some more chips onto the table. With a mix of relief and regret that the incident was over, the other guests around the table took their cue, and restarted their conversations.

Alexei Constantin did not move. For a long, oppressive moment Eve saw him continue to look down at her father. He was very still.

The stillness of a predator before it struck…

The cold pooled again in Eve's stomach.

This man is dangerous…

Deadly.

The words had formed before she could stop them.

Did she move? Did she make a noise, however suppressed, in her throat? She didn't know.

All she knew was that suddenly, out of nowhere, Alexei Constantin's gaze shifted.

Lifted to her.

And froze.

Shock ripped through him. Shock and something much, much worse.

He let his eyes rest on her. Deliberately did so. Forcing himself.

He had not gone after her. Had not called her back. Had let her run.

Because it was not the time. Not the place. He was too close, too close to his goal. Too close to the moment he had spent his adult life determined, striving, to reach.

The moment when Giles Hawkwood would be destroyed.

And nothing, nothing on this earth, in this life, could get in the way of that.

Not even a woman whose beauty was like no other he had ever seen, who had drawn him as no other woman ever had, who had touched him as no other had.

Who had kissed him in the velvet night, with moonlight in her hair…

And who had run from him. Unknown. Unnamed.

Until this moment.

The moment that had revealed her for who she was.

Eve Hawkwood. The daughter of the man he was about to destroy.

He went on looking at her. She returned his gaze. It was as blank as his.

Then, as if a knife had cut him down, he turned and walked away.

Eve Hawkwood.

Alexei said the name again in his head. Letting the two words bore through his brain.

It had to be her. Doing the social honours for Giles Hawkwood.

Social honours? Alexei's mouth twisted savagely. Anger bit through him. Black and roiling. It had been breeding in him since the moment shock had ripped through him as he had looked at the woman behind Giles Hawkwood's chair and realised who she was.

What she was.

And what she was, he knew, with the black anger biting through him, was good. Very good.

He had to give her that.

Skilful in the extreme.

She had played it with an expertise that was unequalled. Every little touch had been perfect.

The pose by the entrance to the casino, the perfectly timed eye-contact, the pause, and then the equally perfectly timed flight to the romantically deserted garden.

And then…

No. He wouldn't allow himself to think about 'and then'.

It had never happened. He had never kissed her. Never kissed her with moonlight in her hair, and cool, soft silk on her lips. Never felt that strange, inexplicable emotion so deep within him that he could not tell what it was, unknown, mysterious, like the woman he'd thought he was kissing…

Who had been someone else entirely all along.

He walked on out of the casino. In the lobby, he cast around. He needed a drink.

Somewhere dark, where he could be left alone.

Without missing a beat he headed for the broad swathe of stairs that led not up, but down, down to the hotel's nightclub in the basement. That would do him fine.

Alexei Constantin.

That was who her fantasy was—the man hunting down her father's company. Bitter irony pierced Eve. Of all the men, in all the world, her dream man was Alexei Constantin...

But even if he hadn't been it would not have made any difference, she knew, with a sagging of her shoulders in defeat. She would still have had to run, like Cinderella, from a ball she could never go to. Condemned to the only life she had, never to seek escape again.

A voice pierced her bleakness.

'*Cherie,* you are not thinking about me—I can tell. If you were, you would look happier.'

Eve gave an apologetic moue.

'I'm sorry, Pierre. I'm not very good company tonight.'

'*Tant pis*—I shall make you smile, and then I shall take you to bed.'

A reluctant twitch formed at Eve's mouth. Pierre Roflet had been trying to take her to bed ever since she'd known him, and right now she was glad of his company. He'd sauntered up to the roulette table half an hour ago, exclaiming at finding Eve here in the South of France unannounced, and swiftly removed her to the nightclub below the casino. Her father had turned briefly, seen who it was, and nodded his permission.

Eve had gone with Pierre with relief. She'd wanted only to return to the yacht, but she knew her father would not permit it until he was ready to go, and that could be some hours away. His luck, so it seemed, had finally turned at the roulette table.

So instead she was whiling away the time to the throb of music in the dimly lit nightclub, with Pierre to distract her. He was amusing, very lightweight, but not unkind. And right now she could do with some amusing, kind and lightweight company.

She'd let Pierre dance with her once, then retired to a table set among armchairs, letting Pierre rattle on with gossipy anecdotes and bestow over-the-top compliments on her. She'd sipped coffee and felt some of the bleakness drain from her.

Yet even so, now, when Pierre had abandoned her to order another coffee and a cocktail, she felt it returning. Blankly, she gazed out over the crowded dance floor. So many couples— some permanent, most temporary. While she…

For a few pointless moments she let her imagination go where it wanted. To the fantasy that had her in its grip. Out over the dance floor, to where she would be, her hands at the nape of his neck, her head resting on his chest, his hands resting lightly, oh so lightly, at her waist…

Sharply, she set aside her fantasy. Indulging it would only feed it, and what was the point of that? None. None at all.

'Dance with me.'

Her head whipped round. Shock widened her eyes. Her heart surged in her chest. Her mouth dried like a desert.

Alexei Constantin stood there, holding out a hand to her.

'Dance with me,' he said again.

His eyes were dark. Very dark. She could not see their pupils.

Like a sleepwalker she put her hand in his, and felt his fingers close over hers. A frisson jarred through her. He drew her to her feet.

He did not look at her. Simply walked her out on to the dance floor.

And put his arms around her.

Her hands splayed against his chest, slipping past the lapels of his jacket to press against the fine, warm surface of his dress shirt. She felt his breath still a moment, then his breathing resume. Beneath her palms she felt the smooth hard muscle beneath the thin material.

Heat flared through her body, out along her cheekbones. She couldn't look at him. Couldn't look at all. Could do nothing except let his hands on her back steer her, in a slow, sensual rhythm, into the dance.

Time stopped.

Everything stopped. Except what was happening to her now. But only for now.

She shut her eyes and let her forehead lower slowly, until it was resting on him.

And then she danced with Alexei Constantin.

He was insane, he knew. Every brain cell in his head told him that. He was insane to have gone anywhere near her again. Insane to have watched her, *à deux* with Pierre Roflet.

Watched Eve Hawkwood in action.

Pierre Roflet. Son of the president of a French investment bank that could, if Roflet *père* so chose, provide sufficient financial muscle to shore up Hawkwood and fend off the takeover.

A very suitable target for Eve Hawkwood's skills.

Was that why he had done what he had? To give Roflet *fils* a chance to escape her toils? Even as the words formed, he knew them for a lie. He knew exactly, *exactly* what had made him do what he had just done.

He had wanted, just once more, to have this woman in his arms again. For one last time to enjoy the fantasy of what he had thought she might be. He didn't care that she was nothing but an illusion, unreal. For this last, brief time he would believe the fantasy.

The music throbbed in his blood. Soft, sensual.

Like the woman folded against him.

Her body was so pliant, so slender. Her head bowed against him, her hands resting lightly, oh so lightly, against the wall of his chest. Her hips resting against his.

He could feel his body react, damn it as he might. Instinctively he drew back a little, using what frail shreds of sanity remained to him.

He felt a shimmer go through her, a fine vibration of her spine beneath the tips of his fingers. His eyes swept down over her in the dim, pulsing light. Her hair was so pale, even without moonlight.

He did not mean to, but he could not help himself. Slowly, he dipped his head, letting his mouth graze the fine silk of her hair.

The shimmer came again, the vibration of her body. His fingers tightened on her spine, as if to arch her towards him.

Slowly, infinitely slowly, he circled the dance floor with her. Taking his time.

Savouring the last of his time with her. Before he put her aside for ever.

The music faded to silence. He stopped. His arms started to slip from her.

Slowly, heavily, as if it were the heaviest weight in the world, she lifted her head.

Looked up at him.

Just looked.

And in that moment doubt knifed through him.

Then sanity flooded through him again. He dropped his hands away, stepping back.

Without a word, he walked away.

Eve just stood there. It was all she could do. A knife blade had just slid between her ribs. It was a physical pain.

She turned around, catching her skirt with her fingers, so that she could hurry, stumble, back to her seat. As she did so, Pierre Roflet got to his feet. He must have returned to their table while she was dancing.

Dancing with Alexei Constantin.

Why had he done it? Her question was anguished. Why had he not just left her alone? What had he danced with her for? There was no point. No point at all. So why do it?

Heavily, she sank into her chair.

Pierre Roflet looked at her silently a moment. Then he spoke. 'You know who that is, don't you?' His voice was unnaturally grave.

Eve nodded, biting her lip. 'Yes. He's trying to buy my father's company.'

Pierre nodded, his eyes expressive. 'It's not a good idea, *cherie*. Dancing. Or anything else.'

There was kindness in his voice, as well as warning. For a second she just looked at him, a stricken expression in her eyes. Then slowly, soberly, she inclined her head.

'I know,' she said.

'Sensible girl.' Wordlessly, he pushed her coffee towards her. And a glass of champagne.

With shaky fingers Eve took the glass, and drank from it.

'You'd do better with me, *cherie*. You wouldn't weep in the morning.'

Lightly, he brushed her bare arm with his fingers. Then he started to tell her another gossipy anecdote.

She tried to smile.

It wasn't possible.

Alexei walked back to the bar. His gait was very controlled, his face expressionless. Beneath the mask of his face, emotions roiled like dark waters. He'd been insane, all right, but he'd got his sanity back now. Forced it back. Eve Hawkwood could resume her attentions to her original target.

Was she sleeping with Roflet already? Or was she holding out until Roflet père rode to her father's rescue?

No, don't think about Pierre Roflet enjoying Eve Hawkwood.

The woman he'd wanted was not her. It was an illusion, a fantasy that did not exist. A mirage.

'*M'sieu?*'

The barman was hovering attentively. Alexei gave his order. 'Vodka,' he instructed tersely.

The barman nodded, and turned to pour the drink. He placed it in front of Alexei and watched him knock it back, then replace the glass on the surface of the bar. Silently, he refilled it.

Alexei reached for it, let his fingers curl around the cool edge of the glass, but he did not drink it. Already the first one was burning down his throat. Deadening his senses.

'*Russe?*'

The husky voice at his side was female. He turned his head.

There was a woman sitting on the barstool, nursing a glass of champagne. Young. No more than twenty, perhaps. Low-cut dress with a high hem. A lot of make-up.

Good-looking.

Expensive-looking.

Available-looking.

Alexei's eyes narrowed slightly. Assessingly.

Then he answered her.

As he did so, he saw surprise—and wariness—flicker in her eyes. Then it was gone. Instead, she laid a hand with red-lac-quered nails on his sleeve. She smiled.

Invitingly.

It took Alexei only a handful of minutes to persuade her to come up to his suite with him.

Eve watched him walk out of the nightclub. He was difficult to miss. The woman on his arm had the highest heels possible, and was swaying provocatively in her tight-cut dress that moulded over her bottom, skimming high across her thighs. Her long dark hair waved extravagantly down her back.

Her hand, with its long red nails, curled around Alexei Constantin's forearm with blatant possession.

Eve's hand curled tightly around the stem of her champagne flute. As if to break it.

How many more illusions could she stand seeing destroyed?

Yet one more, it seemed.

Pierre was looking where she watched, her eyes wide and stricken.

'Definitely not a good idea, *cherie,*' he murmured.

She tore her eyes away. She looked down into her champagne glass.

'No,' she agreed. 'You're right. Not a good idea.' Her voice was strained.

She made herself look up, look across at Pierre. He gave a little grimace, half-sympathy, half-warning.

'And a health risk.' He nodded in the direction that Alexei Constantin was walking off in. 'The girl is a hooker.'

Eve stared.

Pierre gave a light shrug. 'I know—they shouldn't let them in here. But they—or their pimps—bribe the staff. And she is one, *cherie,* believe me. She offered me her services when I was getting your drink while you were dancing.' He made another slight grimace. 'She is no doubt most expensive. But then, price is not a problem for Alexei Constantin.'

Eve hardly heard him. The sound of the final shattering of her last illusion drowned him out.

For one last, despairing second she felt herself try to fight against what she was seeing, but she was crushed down. Crushed by the damning reality of who and what the man was.

No one worth wanting. No one worth dreaming over.

Bleakly, she lifted her champagne glass to her lips.

CHAPTER THREE

ALONG the line of the sea's edge, to the south, there was still the glimmer of light. Eve stood at the yacht's rail in the cooling air, looking out to sea, not wanting to see the garish brightness of the shore.

Not wanting to think about the ordeal ahead.

Alexei Constantin was coming to dine with her father. And she would have to do her duty as her father's hostess, be gracious and polite, ensure that the conversation flowed smoothly, that the staff performed to the standard her father required, ensure the evening went well.

How could the evening go well? How could it be anything other than a horrible nightmarish ordeal?

Her hands tightened over the rail. She had spent the previous night tossing and turning in bed, bitter and hopeless and angry with herself—and all day she had dreaded the coming dinner. How could she cope with seeing again the man she had made such a fool of herself over? Engaging in some idealised moonlit tryst, a fleeting kiss, then making her swift flight from the scene of her stupidity? The man who had turned out to be the predator slowly circling her father? A man who, whether he was Alexei Constantin or not, saw nothing wrong in dancing with her one moment, then picking up a prostitute in the space of a handful of minutes and taking her off for some expensive, professionally serviced sex?

But she was going to have to cope with it, she knew. If she tried to pretend she was feeling ill, the repercussions from her father would be severe. Financially punitive. It was the way he controlled her. Threatening to hold back money.

She could not risk that. Not when her father's money was so desperately needed. And for that reason she steeled herself for the ordeal ahead. Her mother had taught her well, because it was how she got through her own life. Her mother's stringent drilling would get her through the evening.

As for her frail, pathetic fantasy—that was dead. Quite dead.

What was the saying in English? thought Alexei, as he started to eat the elaborately prepared food placed in front of him. Take a long spoon when you sup with the devil?

Well, he was supping with the devil tonight, all right. His own personal devil.

But as of tomorrow morning, when the news of AC International's Australian acquisition was made official—giving the *coup de grâce* to Hawkwood's failing fight to remain independent—his devil would finally be exorcised.

The years of calculating, planning, executing, would be over.

Justice would finally be served on Giles Hawkwood.

Oh, it would not be the killing blow, he knew, but he would not need to finish him off. Others would do that. Enemies even more ruthless than he. Serving Hawkwood with the justice he so thoroughly deserved.

But now, while the man did not yet realise his time was up, Alexei could watch him—coldly and silently—behaving as if there were still time to escape, time to do a face-saving deal that would allow him to emerge from this takeover bid with advantage.

Not that he was raising the subject now. No. Now, as Giles

Hawkwood entertained his nemesis, the subject was quite different. It was art. The topic had been picked by Eve Hawkwood.

Alexei rested veiled eyes on her, forcing himself to do so. He wished to God she were not here. Her presence was a distraction, diluting and disturbing his focus on Hawkwood's coming annihilation. Though he'd known she would be at this travesty of a dinner, the reality of seeing her again was worse than he had expected. In the last twenty-four hours he'd ruthlessly refused to let himself think about her.

Yet the first sight of her as he'd walked into the stateroom had made a mockery of his resolution. It had been like a punch to the solar plexus.

It still was. But now he was slamming down hard on his reaction to her. He had to. It was essential. Essential to be able merely to look at her with his eyes veiled, betraying none of the turbulent thoughts within. Refusing to allow her to use her skills on him.

And she was, as she had been the day before, very skilful indeed.

She was wearing cream tonight, another simple column of fine layers of fabric, caught at each shoulder with a pearled clasp. It was a demure design, and yet the impulse that filled him, instantly and insistently, was not a response to the demure design. It was a response that made him want to stride across to her, slide his hands down her bare arms and draw her towards him as he had done last night, in the moonlight, by the sea's edge…

He hauled his mind back from memory and desire.

She was not that woman. That woman was a mirage.

She was Eve Hawkwood, a woman prepared to engage in sex with men chosen for her by her father, for his own financial advantage—and hers.

Not that one would guess it. It was not her cool, untouchable appearance, but her whole manner and demeanour. She sat, poised and graceful, her crystal-cut tones moving effortlessly, smoothly, from one innocuous topic to another as she played the dutiful role of attentive dinner party hostess. Making not one reference, by sign or by word, to what had happened not twenty-four hours ago, when he had kissed her in the moonlight.

It was as if it had never happened.

But then, of course—his mouth twisted briefly—what he had thought had happened, had not. All that had really taken place was that Eve Hawkwood had, whether opportunistically or calculatedly, tried out her wiles on him.

Well, she wasn't trying them out tonight—not in that way, at any rate. Tonight a different Eve Hawkwood was on show. The society hostess—a role she executed to perfection.

She had already exhausted the flora and fauna, folk customs and natural features of Dalaczia, and had now moved on to art.

'Do you collect art, Mr Constantin?' came the polite enquiry, with a slight lift of her eyebrow in his direction as she gracefully forked up a mouthful of sole Veronique.

'No,' he replied.

It was almost true. He owned only one work of art—a Dutch still life of flowers. Though small, scarcely more than the size of a computer screen, its tumbling, vibrant blooms painted in exquisite detail so that minute ladybirds were visible on leaves and drops of water gleamed on petals, it was like an icon to him.

Ileana had loved flowers...

For a moment the pain was as harsh as ever.

He could see again, so vividly, so real, the way her dark fall of hair had caught the sunlight as she'd picked a meadow flower and given it to him—the smile on her face the one that was just for him, her special smile...

No—the steel door slammed down, impenetrable to all memory, all pain.

Forcibly, he turned his mind back to where he was now—the present. The past was gone; it would never come back. The present was now. And the future—the future would bring justice. That was all he asked of it.

'It doesn't appeal to you, art?' Eve Hawkwood's crystal tones came again.

Alexei reached to lift the glass of vintage wine to his mouth.

'Art is not for private consumption or financial investment,' he replied tersely.

He watched her raise delicate eyebrows at his assertion.

'An admirably purist view,' she responded.

Pure? What did Eve Hawkwood know of pure? Derision curled in Alexei. A sudden desire to pierce her appearance of demure untouchability—so deceptive, so deceiving—possessed him.

'Besides—' he looked straight at her '—so much art was commissioned as pornography—Louis XV of France liked to see his mistresses naked on canvas for his private pleasure.'

Not a flicker showed in Eve Hawkwood's eyes at his deliberately provocative remark. She merely maintained an expression of polite but indifferent interest in a guest's conversation.

'The decadence of Louis XV's private life must certainly have been a factor in the growing disillusion with the French monarchy in the eighteenth century,' she merely observed concurringly, and paused to request some more mineral water from a steward.

'Talking of nudes, Constantin.' Giles Hawkwood's heavy tones suddenly interjected into the pause, as he swivelled his head towards his guest. 'I've got a private film collection of my own I can show you. Every colour and size of girl to suit all tastes—as many as you like at a time, in any combination. I had them filmed to my own specification. Acts like a catalogue—they all work for the same agency, and I fly them in when I want them. The agency gets fresh girls all the time—never delivered a dud yet.' He leant back heavily in his chair, taking a large mouthful from his glass of wine, from which he'd been drinking freely all evening. 'Last time they sent me a woman who could do things with her thighs you wouldn't think physically possible!' He gave a crack of crude laughter. 'You should come along some time—I'll organise something special for you. Something really memorable.'

Another crack of laughter came from him, and he drained his glass, signalling to the steward to refill it. While the man was pouring, Giles Hawkwood looked across at his guest with pouched eyes.

'You'll have to tell me what you like, Constantin. I can lay on any type of girl you want—and any equipment and accessories you enjoy. All top quality. Just say the word.'

He started to drink from his refilled glass.

Alexei's face had stilled. Drained of all expression.

He felt his fists start to curl—felt murderous rage sear through him.

No! He would not soil his hands on Giles Hawkwood. The man was dead meat already—he simply did not know it yet.

Forcibly, with rigid self-control, he made his hands relax. To his left he saw from the edge of his vision that Eve Hawkwood was continuing with her meal. His eyes turned to her. She was cutting a piece of lamb on her plate, and it was as if nothing exceptional had been said at all, as if she were perfectly at ease as the subject of her father's sexual proclivities arose.

And yet—

There was a rigidity in her jaw that was almost imperceptible, but Alexei could detect it all the same. A momentary glazing of her eyes, as if she were shutting something out of her consciousness.

Then, as she proceeded to spear the chunk of meat with her fork, she remarked, 'I can remember reading an article once— it was quite serious, I believe—about how one could use nude portraiture as a guide to the nutritional habits of the societies that produced those works of art. It might have been pretentious, but I suppose it must be true, after all. Who considers Rubens' rotund females to be healthy these days?'

There was just the right amount of light humour in her voice, just the right amount of amused questioning. It would have served just as well if she'd been talking to a bevy of bishops or a division of dowagers.

Did she think she was going to get an answer? Alexei's eyes narrowed even more. Then, abruptly, he spoke. It was an impulse that came from somewhere he thought had ceased to exist in relation to Eve Hawkwood.

But it was something to do with the punishing rigidity of her throat, the blankness in her eyes, the visible whiteness around her fingernails as she lifted and lowered her fork. The jerkiness with which she was eating her lamb.

She was hiding it, but Eve Hawkwood's stress levels were sky-high.

Why?

There was only one reason. Could only be one reason.

Because Eve Hawkwood was as repulsed by her father as he was.

Alexei's eyes were riveted to her.

Was that it? Was that what was going on behind that flawless composure, that social surface that Englishwomen of her class presented to the world as effortlessly as they cut their vowels on crystal?

Except that now, right now, it wasn't effortless. The fan of tension around her eyes, the rigidity of her expression. That required effort. Effort to maintain.

His eyes narrowed fractionally.

What was going on under that blank surface?

And suddenly, as he started to speak, he felt emotion spear through him.

Was I wrong about her? Is she not her father's creature after all?

And if she weren't—if Eve Hawkwood weren't what those surreptitious rumours about her said she was, if she didn't select her lovers from those men whom her father instructed her to, for his own ends—then maybe, just maybe, what had happened last night, that extraordinary, consuming moment of insanity that had possessed him, that had made him follow after her, seek her out, claim her—kiss her—was not an illusion at all...

The emotion speared him again. He did not know what it was. He had never felt it before.

But it was powerful. Very powerful.

And, because of that, he needed to control it. Absolutely. Totally. Completely.

So as he spoke he pitched his voice to match her own.

'Health and beauty do seem to be in opposition these days. Obesity was relatively rare in the past, as it still is in much of the non-western world. In the west the opposite holds true,' he contributed dryly.

He watched her give a slight smile to acknowledge his comment, and saw the web of tension around her eyes slacken minutely as the conversation reverted to acceptable topics.

'Indeed,' she responded, picking up on his remark. 'We're obsessed with thinness—to the detriment of our health.'

Alexei lifted his glass.

'You, however, succeed in achieving the perfect medium— as rare as that is.' He tilted his wine glass in a swift and silent toast, his eyes resting on her, taking in, whether he wanted to or not, the slender but softly rounded curves of her body, veiled by the creamy layers of her dress, and all the more exquisite for it. It enhanced so subtly the extraordinary beauty she possessed. And suddenly, without his volition, the iron guard he had imposed on himself all evening dropped.

It was only for a fraction of a moment, but it was enough. The damage had been done. He had let something show; he knew he had. Something that had been in his eyes last night as he'd approached her, as she'd stood pooled in moonlight beneath the scented pines, remote, beautiful, drawing him to her as no other woman had ever done...

His guard had dropped because she'd made him doubt what he knew about her, made him question his judgement of her.

Which is she? The woman I first thought her or her father's corrupt creature, using her body for his ends?

The question burned through him. He had to know—

His eyes went on resting on her, letting her see what had been in his eyes the first time he had seen her, silver-framed in the entrance to the casino, pure and beautiful. *Was that a lie?* Suddenly, it was the most important question in the world.

Eve set down her wine glass. It took all her self-control. But then every moment of this excruciating evening had required every bit of her hard-won self-control. Only by imposing total discipline on herself was she getting through it.

Her mother, she knew, would be proud of her.

Nothing, absolutely nothing of what she was feeling was showing. And that was essential. Utterly essential.

Seeing Alexei Constantin again was disastrous. She had acknowledged that in the first moment he'd walked into the stateroom, and she'd had to glide forward and take his hand in greeting. Not to have done so would have been socially unacceptable, because he was her father's guest and she, whatever else she would have given years of her life to be, was her father's hostess.

But even as the cool, long fingers had closed over hers, so very briefly, she'd known she should have done the socially unacceptable, however much her rigid training had told her never, never to do so. Because simply touching his hand, so fleetingly, had been disastrous. Disastrous because instantly, though she'd tried to fight it, she had been there, once again, out in the hotel's gardens, in the moonlit darkness, alone with a man who—

Who wants your father's company and who buys sex.

The cruel, condemning words were like stones, crushing her. Crushing hope. Making a mockery of memory.

But memory mocked her still, had mocked her all evening as she'd sat at her father's table making endless small-talk, as a good hostess should. And now it was more than memory that mocked her.

How could she be so helplessly aware of Alexei Constantin as to want to do nothing more than gaze at him, drink in the planes of his face, the line of his mouth, the dark, chill pools of his eyes? How could she be so punishingly aware of the way his long fingers curved around the stem of his wine glass, the way his sable hair feathered on his brow, the way his high cheekbones flared beneath the dark, veiled orbs of his long-lashed eyes, the way the lines about his mouth indented into his tanned skin, the way the superb cut of his tuxedo sat perfectly across the lean breadth of his shoulders…?

How could he still make her heart beat like a wild bird in a cage, even though she knew who he was—what he was?

It was a torment. Exquisite and punishing.

Shaming and humiliating.

To still be affected by the appearance of a man, even while she knew what he was. A man cut from the same cloth as her father, tainted by the same loathsome vice.

Only one final humiliation was spared her. He had made no reference, given her no reminder, of what she had so stupidly done the night before. There was nothing at all of the way he had locked her eyes to his in the entrance to the casino, or the way he'd advanced on her, with purpose and intent, out in the gardens, or even the way his eyes had rested on her as he'd taken her off onto the dance floor in the nightclub.

There was nothing, absolutely nothing, of that.

And then out of nowhere, he'd made that remark about her appearance. Had looked at her. Locked his eyes to hers.

Devastatingly. Disastrously.

She had had no time to prepare against it.

Another emotion had been uppermost in her conscious

mind—an emotion she had not expected to feel about Alexei Constantin.

Gratitude. Numb, dumb gratitude that he had followed her conversational cue after her father had made his vile, repulsive and churningly embarrassing invitation to participate in one of his 'parties'.

She hadn't thought to wonder why Alexei Constantin had not taken up the invitation, had only cast about—desperately—for some bland remark she could make to return the conversation to an acceptable topic, to continue with this punishing farce of an evening.

A wave of sick weariness washed over her. If she could just get through the rest of the meal, then at last she would be able to escape to her cabin.

Escape from her father.

And, even more imperatively, escape from the man who was nothing more than a cruel mockery of the foolish, hopeless, unattainable fantasy she had so briefly thought him to be.

Alexei sat back in his chair, an almost empty wine glass playing in his fingers. He was alone, finally, with his prey. Giles Hawkwood had dismissed his daughter along with the stewards at the end of the meal, slipped the buttons on his dinner jacket, and leaned back more heavily in his seat, reaching into the humidor at his right to select a cigar and clip the end. The crystal port decanter was already at his left. Alexei had refused any, indicating that he preferred to finish his wine.

He had watched Eve Hawkwood walk away, taking her polite leave, graceful and gracious to the last. His eyes had followed the straight line of her back, the way the lamplight caught the pale coil of hair at the nape of her neck, how the folds of her gown graced the slender length of her legs. He'd been struck by her elegant beauty. Could she really be as corrupt as her father?

Was the appearance the truth or the lie?

The question tormented him. Even now, as Giles Hawkwood, with his corrupt pouched eyes, set out his final bid to save his doomed skin—a face-saving merger, not an outright acquisition.

Alexei could have laughed in his face.

But he knew that if he made any move at all it would not be to laugh. It would be to reach forward, dump his wine glass on the table, close his hands around Giles Hawkwood's throat and choke the life out of him—

Instead, he went on sitting there, his eyes veiled, long lashes half swept down, letting Hawkwood spell out the complex web of share structure he was proposing. Holding companies and nominees and multiple tiers of ownership and voting stock, and disparate listings on a range of stock exchanges so complex it would send auditors into a tailspin. But, for all the complexity and financial sophistication, it all boiled down to one thing and one thing only. Giles Hawkwood was trying to keep his company under his own personal control as his own personal empire.

Alexei did not listen. Not just because Giles Hawkwood was already beyond salvation, but because something other than his prey's destruction was occupying his mind.

Is she her father's daughter? How can I know for sure…?

The question obsessed him, going round and round in his brain as Giles Hawkwood laid out his labyrinthine scheme for evading the fate Alexei had set for him. A fate which, clearly, he would do anything to avoid.

Anything?

Alexei stilled. Just what *was* Giles Hawkwood prepared to do to save his skin? Suddenly, Alexei knew exactly how to find out the truth about Eve Hawkwood.

Deliberately, he waited until the moment was right. Then, taking a slow, ruminative mouthful of his wine, he spoke.

'A merger,' he said, his veiled eyes resting on Giles Hawkwood's face, 'would require more than share-swaps and mutual cross-holdings of stock, whatever the composite corporate structure.'

He paused. Giles Hawkwood's expression had changed. Minutely, but perceptibly. Alexei almost allowed himself a vicious smile. The man thought his bait was being taken. Well, let him think that for a few minutes longer.

Giles Hawkwood's eyes narrowed in their pouches.

'Go on,' he said. There was a watchfulness about him, a tension he sought to hide. But, given the amount of alcohol he had so unwisely consumed that evening, to Alexei it was rife in the set of his jowled face.

'There's one asset you possess that you haven't put into play yet.' Alexei's voice was low, controlled.

Giles Hawkwood absently swirled the brandy in his glass.

'Enlighten me.'

Alexei placed his hand flat on the tablecloth, fingers splayed, as he sat, outwardly relaxed, in his chair.

'Your daughter,' he said softly, 'is very beautiful.'

His eyes never left his prey's.

A fat smile started on Giles Hawkwood's face. Alexei could see the satisfaction lighten in his eyes. And less perceptibly, but there all the same, the relief.

'Ah, yes, Eve,' he drawled. 'As you say—very beautiful. Exceptionally so, wouldn't you say?'

His heavy voice was blatant. So was the coat tail he next trailed.

'A…relationship with her…would not be out of place, Constantin, were we to become…partners.'

Alexei's eyes dipped and he gave the slightest shake of his head.

'I'm not the marrying kind—'

There was a brief, coarse laugh for answer. 'Just the red-blooded kind that likes a good—'

He used a word that came from his mouth as naturally as any euphemism. Alexei said nothing, showed nothing. Merely waited.

Giles Hawkwood drank from his brandy, then settled himself back more comfortably in his chair, his girth pushing at the arms.

'So, Eve's caught your eye, has she? Well, why not? If she weren't my daughter I'd be happy enough to—' He broke off and gave another coarse laugh. Then he reached for another cigar.

His mood had lightened, Alexei could tell. For himself, he could feel the pads of his fingers splayed on the table pressing down into the fine white damask. Emotion was knifing through him, but he was controlling it. Controlling it as tightly as it would be necessary to control the finger pressure on a loaded gun. He chose his next words with infinite care, picking exactly the ones he wanted.

'Oh, she's beautiful, all right. But...' the long lashes swept momentarily down, then back up again '...appearances can be deceptive. Some women are beautiful—but cold. She may be beautiful but...' He paused minutely, his eyes never leaving his prey. 'Is she any good?'

Giles Hawkwood set his cigar down in the ashtray. He looked straight across at Alexei, his shoulders easing. Then he spoke.

There was no hesitation, no reluctance, no evasion.

'Why not go and try her out?' he invited.

She was lying in the bed, her hair loose at last, a pale, moonlit swathe across the pillow. The sheet hardly covered her long, delicate limbs, slanting half exposed. She was wearing some kind of negligee, Alexei could see, but it was nothing more than a swathe of silk, one strap loosened from her shoulder.

She was asleep.

Or at least pretending to be asleep.

He stood for a while, looking down at her. There was no light in the luxuriously appointed cabin, the one that Giles Hawkwood had directed him to, only the pale reflection from the ship's lights playing on the water, reflecting into the room from the uncurtained windows. A breath of air from the sea indicated the windows were open as well as uncurtained.

It was cool in the cabin, cool and quiet, with only the slightest swell of the tideless sea beneath the hull.

He could not even hear her breathe, could only dimly make out the rise and fall of her breasts as she lay, long eyelashes shuttering her grey eyes.

She looked so innocent…so pure…

For a moment something shafted deep inside him. Surely, *surely* no woman could look so beautiful, so innocent—and yet not be so?

But Eve Hawkwood was no innocent. The veil of her beauty was just that—a deception, a lie. The truth was very, very different.

She was a woman prepared to be sexually available to a man her father wanted to appease. The corruption that rotted the man who had fathered her had rotted her as well.

He felt something crawl over his skin.

He had wanted the truth about Eve Hawkwood, and now he had it.

His hand reached out. He watched it do so, of its own volition. He wanted to call it back, but did not. Let it—let him—take one last taste of a woman who would now be beyond temptation.

His palm rounded over her breast. He felt the blood surge in his body, desire leap in his veins. For one exquisite, pleasurable moment he let her breast ripen under his hand, feeling her nipple engorge and strain against his palm. A low moan came from her throat, and he saw her lips part. Her silk-veiled nipple grazed against his skin, teasing at the juncture of his palm and fingers. His blood surged again. He felt his body tighten, flooding through his defences.

He almost succumbed. Almost he lowered himself down beside her, to peel her negligee from her, to expose her swelling breasts, to tweak those hard, ripe nipples with his fingers, to rouse her from her feigned sleep. Because how else could her body be responding to his caress if she were not totally, absolutely conscious of what he was doing? To let his hand slide down the lush length of her silk-clad body, draw that veil up and glide his hand between her parted thighs to seek, and find, the moistening entrance to her body and prepare it for his pleasure…

She gave another low, husked moan in her throat, her eyelids moving over her still-shut eyes. Her body stirred softly, languorously.

Eve Hawkwood was signalling her readiness to make her body available at her father's bidding…

His hand lifted away. Cold drenched through him.

God, but she had nearly succeeded! Nearly drawn him down into her silken web. Nearly made him succumb to her, and what she offered—to him, and to any man her father chose for her.

Abruptly, he stepped away, and turned on his heel. The air in the cabin felt thick suddenly, despite the freshness from the open window. Rank and foul, as if the corruption all around him were choking the air.

He had to get out. Get out of this cabin, out of this place. He should never have come here—never indulged in the baiting of the man he was going to destroy. Doing so, indulging in the savage satisfaction of knowing that his prey had no escape, had been a contamination. A contamination he should never have exposed himself to.

He walked from the cabin, flinging back the door, striding along the wide companionway, back into the stateroom.

Giles Hawkwood was still there. He had poured himself yet more port, lit yet another cigar. He looked sleek, satisfied, relishing his reprieve from ruin. As Alexei walked in he twisted his head, his expression changing. He opened his mouth, ready to speak.

But he got no chance.

Ruthless now. Going straight for the jugular. No more toying with his prey.

Just the swift, killing blow.

'Check the newsfeeds from Sydney. I've just acquired Rencorp. That gives me a clear majority holding in Hawkwood. It's over. You're finished.'

Then he walked from the room.

Justice had at last been done on Giles Hawkwood.

As for his daughter—she was finished too.

CHAPTER FOUR

WARM late-afternoon sunlight filled her mother's sitting room, illuminating the *eau-de-nil* hand-blocked wallpaper, watered silk curtains, delicate eighteenth century antique furniture and carefully chosen *objets d'art*. It was a room, Eve knew, that perfectly suited her mother. A beautiful, elegant refuge from the world.

Now, as her mother mixed herself a gin and tonic—more gin than tonic, Eve noted grimly, she could see the tremble in her hand. She was still in shock—and so was Eve.

Because the unbelievable had happened.

Her father had lost the battle for Hawkwood Enterprises.

She had never believed it would happen. How could it? Her father never lost any battle he undertook—no one ever won against him. Dear God, didn't she and her mother know that? As did everyone else who had ever had any dealings with Hawkwood Enterprises and the man behind it—Giles Hawkwood.

But Giles Hawkwood no longer owned Hawkwood Enterprises. He had lost it—lost the battle for it.

She had discovered it the very next morning, when she had woken up on the yacht. Woken after a dream so disturbing, so terrifyingly potent and real, that it had taken the shock of hearing from the crew that her father had left the vessel—and the reason why—to wipe it from her mind. She had flown straight back to

London, neither knowing nor caring where her father was, and driven west out along the M40, to turn off the motorway and drive along winding roads and increasingly narrow lanes into the heart of the Chilterns, until she had reached the remote, brickbuilt Queen Anne manor house, Beaumont, nestled into a fold of the wooded hills, which was her mother's haven.

Breaking the news to her mother had not been easy, but more had come. The following few weeks had disclosed the full debacle surrounding Hawkwood Enterprises. And as AC International had taken ownership, two things had happened. The Serious Fraud Office had launched an investigation into Hawkwood Enterprises' finances. And Giles Hawkwood had disappeared off the face of the earth.

The scandal had been all over the press and the City. But Eve didn't care about the scandal. She cared about something far, far more important to her.

The gravy train had stopped flowing, just as her father had warned.

After seeing to her mother, that had been Eve's first priority. It had to be. She had contacted her bank, her father's bank, her father's accountant—and they had all said the same thing. There were no more funds. None. Nothing was being paid into her account, or her mother's. Repossession orders had been served on her flat in Chelsea and on her mother's Kensington apartment, both of which had been corporate assets of her father's company—which he no longer owned. Eve and her mother had vacated them, retreating to the sanctuary of Beaumont—all that was left to them. All except the money which Eve had secreted in a bank account that not even her father had known about. It had been squirreled away from the funds her father had paid out to her mother—his means of controlling her, and thereby their daughter too—saved carefully over the years, hoarded and protected.

And invested. Invested in Eve's own personal portfolio, using the business acumen which she had, so ironically, inherited from the father she loathed and despised, and built, little by little, year by year, into a fund which, though nowhere near the amount her father had doled out to her mother, nevertheless was now going to be just enough to keep Beaumont going—if they were careful, if they were prudent and thrifty and penny-pinching.

Eve grimaced impotently. It seemed so bitterly galling that the ridiculously lavish lifestyle she and her mother had lived when they were in London, imposed on them by her father, had been so expensive to maintain, when the money could so much better have gone to Beaumont. Well, that lifestyle was gone.

Just as her father was gone.

That, out of all this debacle, was the only saving grace she was clinging to. Her father was finally gone from their lives. Because surely, with the SFO crawling all over the Hawkwood books, it must mean that her father's financial handling of his company had been so criminally dubious that he would not dare show his face again in the UK?

And if that were so—

Are we free of him? Are we really, truly free of him?

Hope, desperate hope, leapt in her heart.

She looked across at her mother. Her face was etched with worry, but at least she no longer wore the immaculately made-up face the world had always seen her with. Eve's eyes shadowed bleakly. As a teenager she had finally realised just why her mother's make-up was always so perfect, whatever the time of day. Its purpose had not merely been to retain her ageing beauty, but also a much darker reason.

To conceal the bruises on her skin.

Only once, when she was sixteen, had Eve stood up to her father about it. Fury had filled her and she'd threatened her father with the police.

'I'll take photos and prove what you do to her!' she'd raged.

Her father had only laughed contemptuously.

'You stupid little bitch! She'll never testify against me—and she'll never divorce me either!'

Eve had bowed her head and given in. Her mother's abject terror of her husband had been so overpowering that all Eve had been able to do was give her mother as much shelter and protection as she could.

And try, as best she could, to stop her mother seeking shelter and protection from too many gin and tonics…

Now, at last, it might just be that her mother would be free of Giles Hawkwood—and that would mean that Eve was free as well. But the fear built over so many years of abuse was hard to overcome.

'You can start divorce proceedings,' she urged. 'You can cite desertion—now that he's gone that's all you'll need to do.'

Her mother jerked her glass to her lips, her hand shaking.

'No! He's going to come back! I know he will. I *know!* He always comes back. He leaves me alone for ages, and then suddenly he comes back. Late at night—I can't stop him. I can't stop him. I can never stop him!'

Eve could hear the terror in her voice. She took her mother's hand in hers.

'If he comes back, then he will be in custody. The police don't investigate these cases of corporate fraud unless there is a lot of evidence. And from what I read—' her voice sounded stiff suddenly '—the new owners are co-operating fully with the SFO. They don't want any mud sticking to them.'

Her mouth tightened. Alexei Constantin had taken possession of her father's company and promptly summoned the SFO. Had he had any inkling that the company's finances were criminally suspect?

No, don't think about Alexei Constantin. Don't think about anything at all to do with that trip to the Riviera. It belongs to a life that is gone. Gone for good.

And be glad that it's gone!

Yet, for all her admonitions to herself, she felt the memory form yet again in her mind—the memory of standing there alone, in the moonlight, while Alexei Constantin walked towards her…

No! He wasn't who I thought he was. The man I thought he was doesn't exist. He was just a fantasy—a poor, stupid fantasy.

The real Alexei Constantin had shown himself when he'd walked out of that nightclub with a prostitute on his arm. That was all she had to remember about Alexei Constantin…

And anyway, he belonged to a world that now had nothing more to do with her. A world that finally, after so many years, she had escaped.

She closed her eyes in gratitude. She had dreamt of living a life free of her father, and now she had that. So did her mother. And so, too, finally—

She broke her chain of thoughts. Her mother's hand had clenched in hers.

'Eve! I'm frightened—so frightened!'

Immediately she put her arms around her mother's thin body.

'It's all right, it's all right,' she said soothingly. 'He can't hurt you any more. He can't do any more harm.'

Carefully she let go, removing, as she did so, the glass from her mother's shaking hand.

'Everything is going to be all right. Beaumont is safe. Quite safe. I told you I'd put some money aside. It won't be as much as before, but we can manage. We'll have to be careful, it's true, but there'll be enough. I promise you.' She kissed her mother's drawn cheek. 'It's all going to be all right, I promise.'

But her mother jerked away from her. Her eyes were wide and terrified.

'It *isn't*—it isn't all right! It's all wrong. Oh, God, Eve—you don't know. You don't know!'

Cold pooled in Eve's stomach. The terror in her mother was

far more than the fear that her brutal husband would return, that there would be insufficient money from now on.

'What is it?'

'It's Beaumont!'

Eve looked at her mother. 'What do you mean?' she asked carefully.

Her father could not touch Beaumont. Her mother had inherited the house from her family, and it had always been her own possession. Her father had owned the flats in Chelsea and Kensington—moving them, as Eve had discovered, on to the company balance sheet in order to bolster the corporate assets against which to raise money to fight the takeover. But Beaumont he'd been unable to touch.

Yet her mother was trembling. Shaking all the way through her frail, thin body. Eve watched, hollow-stomached, as her mother reached for her glass and took a jerky swallow. Then looked glassily at her daughter. For a second it looked as though she could not say what she wanted to say, then she managed to get it out, her face stricken.

'I made Beaumont over to your father. He said he needed it for the company. To fight off the takeover.'

It was strange, thought Eve, how just when you thought the prison door had opened, an earthquake swallowed you up. Emotion welled in her. Overwhelmed her.

'*How?* How could you do that? How could you hand over this house to him?'

Even as the words burst from her she would have done anything to have recalled them. But it was too late. Her mother flinched as if her daughter had struck her, gin and tonic splashing on her hand.

'He said he needed it,' she said in a toneless voice, devoid of all emotion. 'He said he'd paid for everything. He said if I wanted the money to keep coming, then I had to give him Beaumont. He said it had only survived because of his money. He said I had no right to it. He said I had no right to anything. That I was useless and worthless and spineless and gutless and—'

Eve folded her in her arms.

'Don't—please don't.' Her voice was anguished. She couldn't bear to hear.

Her mother's voice was rising. 'He made me give it to him. He *made* me. He hit me, and hit me, and hit me—until I signed the form he'd brought with him. Oh, God, Eve, he *made* me give it to him.'

Eve held her close, and her mother wept in her arms. Inside, rage consumed her.

And despair.

If Beaumont no longer belonged to her mother, they were lost. Somehow she had to get Beaumont back.

Too much depended on it.

Halting briefly, Alexei reset the timer on the treadmill for another thirty minutes, and started running again. He could feel sweat trickling down his back and beading in his hair. A driving, burning restless energy consumed him. It angered him that it did so.

He shouldn't be feeling like this. He should be feeling that at last the mission that had driven him all of his life had finally been accomplished.

Giles Hawkwood was finished.

And Ileana had her justice.

Pain pierced through him. Ileana, who had left his side as a young girl, scarcely eighteen, and never returned.

Nor would Giles Hawkwood return. Although AC's due diligence on Hawkwood Enterprises had revealed nothing criminal, Alexei had his own sources of information on what had been going on in Giles Hawkwood's company. The moment he had full access to the books—and the figures behind the books—he'd had the confirmation he'd required. He'd invited the SFO in and co-operated fully with their enquiries. As for Giles Hawkwood, he had done exactly what Alexei had known he would do. Bolted for cover.

But he wouldn't find any. Giles Hawkwood, Alexei knew grimly, had done shady business with even shadier people—and such people did not look kindly on those who allowed their murky operations to come to light. They would not welcome with open arms the man who had allowed his company to fall into unfriendly hands.

No, Giles Hawkwood was finished—and not just financially.

It should be, thought Alexei grimly, a good feeling. Closure after so many years. Getting justice for Ileana—peace for himself.

Yet he was not at peace. Was it because his whole life had been spent burning with anger for Ileana's fate? The fate she had met at the hands of the man he had just destroyed. But he could not bring her back; he knew that. He could not give her the life she should have had. All he could do was what he had done—what he was still doing. The fortune he'd made, his weapon of destruction against Giles Hawkwood, could now, at last, be put to other use. He had known that all along, and had looked forward to the day when it was so. That day had now come—yet he could not move forward.

And he knew why. Knew what had at the very last moment, in the very hour of his final revenge over Giles Hawkwood, come between him and the peace of mind he had sought all his life.

A woman stood between him and the peace he sought. Not Ileana, not her poor, avenged ghost, but another woman.

The daughter of the man who had destroyed Ileana.

Eve Hawkwood.

The name, the image, burned in his mind, his inner vision.

And he could not free himself of it.

He had tried. Oh, he had tried! Using all his self-discipline, all his self-control, to exorcise her. But it had not worked. Nor had more practical measures. He had, in the weeks since he had acquired Hawkwood Enterprises, made himself seek out other beautiful women, all of whom had been more than eager to be chosen by him.

None had been able to banish Eve Hawkwood's pale deceptive beauty from his mind.

None had tempted him as she did.

The realisation burned like acid in him.

He started to run faster, punishing the body that wanted a woman he could not have, must not want.

Too corrupt for his touch. But who haunted him. Tormented him.

CHAPTER FIVE

LONDON in early summer was at its best. In late afternoon the fresh green leaves of the trees in the parks and squares were bathed in sunshine. Eve's low-heeled shoes clicked on the stone flagway as she walked along the quiet Mayfair street lined with neatly elegant Georgian houses in which had once dwelt the aristocratic, fashionable throng of the eighteenth and nineteenth centuries. Now nearly all the houses were expensive shops or offices, including the one that she was heading for. The London headquarters of AC International.

Her heart was tight in her chest. Thumping like a hard, tight drum.

She did not want to do this. With all her being, she did not want to do this.

But she had no choice.

In her desperation and despair over Beaumont, after learning that it no longer belonged to her mother, that her father's brutality had wrenched it from her, Eve had had to gather all her strength, all her resources. Somehow she had to get Beaumont back.

But how?

Fear had eaten into her. The funds she had squirreled away and invested were enough to generate income—but if she sold them then there would be no more income. Would the capital raised even be enough for what Beaumont was worth? It would be useless, she knew, to ask her mother's cousin—the present Viscount Duncaster—for help. He was currently embroiled in a bid to save his own financially straitened estates—he was in no position to help her mother. Then, out of the blue, her mother's maternal aunt, her Great-Aunt Marian, had phoned.

And thrown a lifeline which Eve had grabbed with both hands—and an outpouring of gratitude. Her great-aunt had responded in her familiar robust fashion.

'Your mother was an imbecile to marry that brute, but she was to be my beneficiary anyway, so she might as well have the money now, when she needs it. And I devoutly hope we've seen the last of your father, Eve,' she'd finished roundly. 'Now, stop thanking me, my girl, and go and bank the cheque I'm sending you. Then go and buy Beaumont back for your mother.'

Eve's eyes flickered. Buy Beaumont back for her mother?

Could it really be that easy?

She had no idea—none. All she knew was that what she was about to do now was something she would have paid a thousand pounds—ten thousand!—not to have to do. Because when she had written, in a strictly formal fashion, to Hawkwood's new owners, requesting to repurchase a property that had become part of the company's assets, the reply had appalled her.

It had come from the UK executive PA to the chairman of AC International, and informed her that she had an appointment with him for this afternoon.

Why? That was the question that had gone round and round in her head ever since the letter had arrived the previous week. *Why* did Alexei Constantin want to deal with this in person? It made no sense! It was something his finance department would deal with—or his facilities management department—anyone but the man who owned the company that had recently acquired Hawkwood Enterprises!

Resignation sank through her like a heavy weight. What did it matter *why* her request to repurchase Beaumont was not being dealt with by one of his staff? If this was the only chance she had of buying back Beaumont then, even though she would have given anything not to be heading at this moment to Alexei Constantin's London headquarters to keep her unwanted appointment with him, she was going to have to do it.

Getting Beaumont back was an imperative. It overrode everything. Everything. Especially something as absolutely trivial as not wanting ever to set eyes again on Alexei Constantin.

Liar!

The voice inside her head stabbed like a poisoned stiletto.

Liar to say you never want to set eyes on him again!

Instantly into her beleaguered mind his image leapt. She'd tried not to summon it—not to let it intrude, invade her. She'd been grateful, abjectly so, that the crisis that her father's loss of Hawkwood had triggered had driven him from her mind.

At least during the daytime hours…

By night, though, it was a different matter.

By night he returned to haunt her…taunt her.

Torment her.

That dream—the one I had the last night in France. It seemed so real, so incredibly, devastatingly real—

Memory of the dream shivered through her, quickening her pulse.

I dreamt he was there, by my bed. That he was leaning down towards me, reaching out—touching me, caressing me…

Even now, so many weeks later, she could still feel the heat pooling in her stomach as the raw, powerful impact of that so-disturbing dream reverberated in her yet again, as it did so often, so unstoppably.

She had dreamt the dream again, over and over again. She'd tried not to—even though its impact on her body, her being, was less than the first devastating dream had been. Even so, it was still powerful enough to send its disturbing, sensual echoes through her.

Even now…

No! No, this was madness. Madness to allow herself to think about that dream, to think about Alexei Constantin at all.

He was just a fantasy. He doesn't exist. You know the man who exists! A man like your father—

That was what she must remember now. Must cling to.

That and the overriding imperative that she must get Beaumont back.

With heavy heart she went on walking.

Alexei sat at the antique desk and stared grimly down at the figures in front of him. They were not the cause of his grimness.

Why the hell had he been insane enough to do what he had? Summon Eve Hawkwood into his presence again.

He'd known he was insane the moment he'd instructed his PA to give her an appointment. He should consign Eve Hawkwood to oblivion. Let her rot, like her father.

But he couldn't. The urge, the overwhelming temptation to see her once more had overcome him, and he had yielded to it. Like a fool. Yes, he knew that all right—but it hadn't stopped him doing so. Nor had he cancelled the appointment, as he had been on the point of doing countless times this last week since it had been issued.

He wanted to see her again. Wanted to see once more her cool, pale beauty—the beauty that haunted and tormented him.

Even though he knew it for nothing more than a deceptive surface concealing the corruption beneath.

Nonetheless, he still wanted to see her again.

But—and the question ate into him like slow acid on his skin—what else did he want?

He stared unseeingly at the columns of figures printed out in front of him.

What else did he want from Eve Hawkwood?

That was a question he was not prepared to answer.

Not even to himself.

Least of all to himself.

'Miss Hawkwood, Mr Constantin.'

His PA ushered her inside, announcing her arrival. Eve walked into Alexei Constantin's office, her heart still like that tight, hard drum in her chest.

The room must once have been the main salon of the old, double-fronted Georgian house, Eve thought. Her glance took in elegant proportions, velvet-draped sash windows, a fireplace filled with flowers, and oil paintings on the walls. But what dominated her vision—and the room—was the large oak desk, behind which a tall, familiar figure was getting to his feet with a smooth, fluid movement.

Every pincer in her stomach suddenly pinched simultaneously.

Oh God, he still had the same power over her! The same impact!

Her mouth dried.

Why, why can't I control this reaction to him? Why?

Anguish and anger shot through her in equal proportions. She put both aside. She had to. She was not here to agonise over why her body was so treacherous to her mind, to her sensibility. She was here to buy back Beaumont. Nothing more.

Forcing herself, she walked forward.

You survived that dinner party on the yacht—you can survive this!

She looked, she knew, despite the dryness of her mouth and the tight drumming of her heart, neat and businesslike. Her pale green suit was smart, fashionable, but modestly styled. With a high-necked round collar, a long jacket, a knee-length pencil skirt and sensibly-heeled matching court shoes, her hair in a French pleat and nothing more than discreet daytime make-up, she knew she looked unexceptional.

'Mr Constantin, it's very good of you to see me. Thank you.'

No point saying she would rather be anywhere else than here, that she did not want to be here, had not asked to be here.

'Miss Hawkwood—'

The dark eyes surveying her were inscrutable. She approached, keeping her spine rigid. He seemed taller than she remembered. Or perhaps that was because he was outlined against the windows, his dark, superbly cut business suit giving him an even more formidable air than he had had when he'd been in evening dress. It made him look far more what he was, she realised—a powerful, wealthy businessman. One of the movers and shakers of the financial world. A man whose time, she knew, was as scarce as it was valuable. He wouldn't want it wasted.

'Will you sit down?'

The accent in his voice rippled down her spine. She forced a polite, social smile to her mouth.

'Thank you.' She took the chair he indicated in front of his desk. As she sat, he sat too. She took a brief moment to place her handbag on the floor and cross her legs to regain her poise.

Then she looked up. Doggedly she ignored the tightness in her chest as she made herself look levelly at him.

'My original letter indicated that I wish to repurchase a property which is currently on the books of Hawkwood Enterprises,' she opened.

He had sat back in his chair, his hands resting on either arm. His face was unreadable. He made no reply to her, merely waited. She continued, her voice still crisp and crystal.

'I have a market valuation conducted by a director of one of the country's premier estate agents, which I trust you will find acceptable to confirm a price.'

She reached forward to lift up her bag, and extracted a sealed envelope from it, placing it on the desk in front of Alexei Constantin.

Alexei Constantin did not pick up the envelope. Instead, he simply went on resting his inscrutable gaze on her.

'What is the property?'

His voice was as expressionless as his face.

Eve swallowed. Her throat felt constricted suddenly. This was not easy—not easy at all. But it had to be done.

'It is a small country house called Beaumont, in the Chilterns—a range of hills to the northwest of London. It's currently in use as a clinic, but—'

There was a perceptible stiffening in Alexei Constantin's body—then it was gone.

'A clinic?' His voice was colourless.

'Yes. The valuation I've had prepared—which, of course,' she acknowledged, 'you will wish to verify—allows for its current usage.'

'Tell me—why do you want to buy this property?'

'It belonged to my mother until recently, Mr Constantin. It has only lately become part of Hawkwood's corporate assets. My mother now…regrets…that she made it over to Hawkwood Enterprises.'

Her voice was inexpressive. The sick, blinding rage she felt when she thought of how her father had obtained Beaumont must not show. It was not relevant to this moment. Nothing was relevant, except to stay as calm, as composed as she could, and request Alexei Constantin to return the property.

She took a breath, and continued.

'I will be frank with you, Mr Constantin. The property serves no purpose on Hawkwood's balance sheet except as a capital asset. It was placed on the balance sheet simply to provide another…bulwark…in the recent takeover struggle. For that reason

I am sure your finance directors will make the decision that its most appropriate value to Hawkwood now, post-merger, is to dispose of it and release the equity for more useful investment elsewhere. Selling it to me would be the most expedient means of realising its value. As I say, I am perfectly prepared to pay the market price for the property.' She nodded down at the envelope on his desk.

He still did not look at it. Instead, he merely picked up the phone. In brief, expressionless tones Eve heard him instruct his PA, or so she assumed, to locate in the Hawkwood data a property by the name of Beaumont. Then he replaced the phone.

He looked back across at Eve. She still could not read his expression, yet something suddenly seemed to chill down her spine.

Suddenly, out of nowhere, she felt a sense of dread.

For a moment, as he set down the phone and let his gaze rest on her, Alexei felt his muscles tighten. Deliberately, he relaxed them. All day, he knew, the tension had been circling more tightly in his body, his mind, as the hour of Eve Hawkwood's appointment had approached. Even up to the last minute he had almost cancelled the appointment.

But he hadn't. He had let her arrive, let her walk in here as she had, with her cool, understated English beauty. Very understated. He took in again the modestly styled suit, the low heels, the neat hair and almost complete absence of make-up.

As he had once before, he paid tribute to her skill. The image she projected was designed to be unalluring.

But it failed completely. It was not unalluring at all. The very modesty of the outfit only threw into relief the stunning beauty she possessed—the fine bones of her face, her clear grey-green eyes, the pale sweep of her hair. A beauty that yet again, made the breath still in his throat.

Anger stabbed in his guts.

Why? Why did Eve Hawkwood have to be the woman she was? Her father's daughter, his tool, his willing vessel for his sordid machinations. Even now, after he had been destroyed, disposed of like the garbage he was.

His eyes rested on her, drinking her in like a glass of the finest wine. His face was expressionless, but within his emotions roiled and seethed.

How could a woman who looked the way Eve Hawkwood did—with her cool, pale beauty, her untouchable beauty—be the woman she was? She looked elegant, immaculately groomed, her class evident in every line of her body. As though nothing sordid had ever touched her.

There was a voice speaking in his head. He wanted to silence it, but it would not be silenced. It spoke again, even more insistently. Demanding to be heard.

How do you know she is the woman you say she is? How do you know she was her father's willing tool? How can you be sure?

Scorn withered the voice. Her father had offered her to him on a plate, in her own bed, and he had the evidence of his eyes, the touch of his hand upon her, to know the truth of that!

But the voice forced its way into his consciousness again.

The only truth you know about Eve Hawkwood is that you want her—want her more than any other woman you've ever seen. That the memory of that kiss, the moonlight in her hair, torments you. But that's all you know. How can you be sure she knew you were standing there by her bed, watching her—touching her? Why the hell shouldn't she just have been asleep, the way she looked? She is her father's daughter—but that is not her fault. You imposed your judgement on her—but you don't know, you can't know for sure, if you made the right judgement. You're hanging her for her father's crimes...and her father is gone. Finished with. So why do you keep condemning her without clear and unambiguous proof?

The litany drummed through his mind. He wanted to silence it, but it would be heard, all the same.

Anger stabbed in his mind—and something more than anger. Something more powerful.

Very well. If he had misjudged her, if her scum of a father had simply taken a last, desperate gamble to ward off disaster and offered his daughter to him without her knowledge—assuming, no doubt, that he would simply ravish her without her consent—because that, of course, was what Giles Hawkwood would have done in those circumstances!—he could find out the truth easily enough. If he were condemning her for her father's crimes, then he would see if she would commit any of her own volition. Her father was gone now—she was a free agent. Free to do what she wanted—make her own choices.

His mouth hardened. So what choices would Eve Hawkwood make when she was a free agent?

He would offer her one very clear, very unambiguous choice.

And then he would know, once and for all, if she was free from her father's taint—or not.

He felt the tension in him constrict.

On the outcome of her choice more was riding than he wanted to think about. Much, much more.

Abruptly he spoke, getting to his feet.

'I have a conference call due shortly. We'll discuss this matter further over dinner.'

Eve stared at him, consternation in her face. 'Dinner?' she echoed blankly.

'Yes. The Arlington at—' he glanced at his watch, a slim band of gold snaking around his lean wrist, offset by the gleaming white of his cuff '—let us say, nine o'clock.'

He started to walk to the door with long strides, clearly terminating the interview. Eve got to her feet, dismay still drenching through her. She didn't want dinner with Alexei Constantin! She wanted to buy back Beaumont, that was all.

'I'm afraid dinner's quite impossible tonight.'

She heard herself speak, her tone clipped. She hadn't meant it to sound quite so clipped, but it was too late now. Claws were clipping away in her stomach, and they made her voice sharp.

Alexei Constantin had reached the door to his PA's office. He turned. His eyes swept over her.

'If you have a prior engagement, break it. That is unless you no longer wish to continue this discussion.'

I don't want to discuss it at all, she wanted to shout. I just want you to sell me back my mother's house because she needs it desperately, and so do—

She subsided. What was the use? Men as rich as Alexei Constantin did what they wanted, when they wanted to. She'd seen her father crack his whip over his underlings often enough to know that.

Schooling herself, she put a polite, social smile on her face and started to head for the door he was opening to get rid of her.

'Of course. You said nine o'clock at the Arlington, I believe?'

'Yes. Until then—'

She walked past him, out into the outer office. His PA was still there, dutifully working at her PC.

'Miss Hawkwood is leaving,' Alexei told the woman.

Then, without further conversation, he went back to his desk, closing the office door behind him with a snap.

Numbly, Eve left the building.

CHAPTER SIX

FRUSTRATION scraped through her. And more than frustration. The last thing she wanted was to have dinner with Alexei Constantin! Why on earth couldn't he just tell her straight off whether he would or would not sell back Beaumont to her? And why shouldn't he sell it back to her anyway? She was offering a fair price, and he had no use for the place, while she…

No, she couldn't think of just how essential it was for her mother to get Beaumont back. Because if she did her nerves would shred to pieces at the thought that Alexei Constantin might refuse to sell it.

But why *should* he refuse?

The same old pointless worry went round and round in her head, and continued to do so for the next few hours, while she passed the time aimlessly waiting for nine o'clock to finally arrive. After phoning home and leaving a message for her mother to say that she would either be back very late or would stay the night in town, she idly wandered the shops that still had late-night opening. Briefly she considered whether to buy something more suitable to wear for dinner at one of the West End's best hotels, but decided against it. She didn't want to have dinner with Alexei Constantin, and she didn't want to waste money she couldn't afford any more on clothes her new lifestyle meant she did not need. Already the clothes she had bought to be her father's hostess were hanging idle in her wardrobe, swathed in plastic wraps and unworn since the South of France.

No, don't think about the South of France. Don't think about that last excruciating meal with Alexei Constantin on the yacht. Don't think about Alexei Constantin at all. You're going to have dinner with him, hand him your cheque for Beaumont, and get out.

That's all.

That's all you have to do.

Steeling herself, she hailed a taxi.

'The Arlington, please,' she said.

Her expression, as she took her seat in the cab, was tense.

It got tenser still when, on arriving at the Arlington Grill at one minute past nine o'clock, she was informed that there was no reservation that evening for Mr Constantin. Frowning, Eve crossed to the concierge's desk. Five minutes later her tension levels had rocketed sky-high. Mr Constantin, so the concierge had informed her with the polite blandness that she was used to in such places, was expecting her in his suite. A bellboy conducted her there, and as Eve handed him his tip—a note she would rather not have had to expend—she was shown inside.

Yet even as the tension raced in her at the thought of having to dine in a private suite with Alexei Constantin, one part of her could not help but be relieved. To have had to endure the ordeal of dining in one of the most notable restaurants in London with the man who had fought her father so bitterly for his company— her father who was now under criminal investigation—would have been an ordeal she would not have enjoyed.

Not that she would enjoy this ordeal either, but at least it was away from the prying eyes of gossip-obsessed other diners. Here, at least, there was only the hotel's waiting staff, who would never show anything other than bland courtesy as they witnessed her ordeal.

The service would surely be faster, too, and that would mean that she had a better chance of making the last train from Marylebone. Deliberately forcing herself to dilute the tension racing through her, she accepted a drink from the cocktail waiter and glanced around the suite's dining room. The Arlington wasn't a hotel she knew—it was too old-fashioned for her father's tastes—but she found that she liked the discreet, understated elegance of the decor and what she could tell was genuine antique furniture.

She was just smoothing her fingers along the soft patina of the mahogany dining table when a low, accented voice made her start.

'Miss Hawkwood—'

Alexei Constantin was walking into the room. Eve's stomach clenched, and deliberately she forced herself to unclench it. It didn't matter—it didn't matter that every time she laid eyes on Alexei Constantin it was like an electric shock through her. She was here for one reason only—to buy back Beaumont.

Nothing else mattered. Least of all her stupid, pointless reaction to the man who now owned it.

Gathering her poise around her, she gave a small, correct smile and murmured, 'Mr Constantin,' back to him.

'Will you sit down?'

His voice was smooth, urbane—and yet it still sent the blood creaming in her veins.

No—she mustn't, *mustn't* react to him!

Yet as she took her place, her eyes went to him as he seated himself across the table from her.

Like a sheet of emotion, a sudden longing pierced through her out of nowhere, instantly dissolving the guard she had erected against him.

If only she were here, dining with Alexei Constantin, for any other reason! If only he were not the man she knew him to be!

If only she were here because he was, after all, despite her knowledge to the contrary, the man who had taken her breath away with her very first sight of him! If only they were dining together *à deux* for the very first time…

A private suite, candlelight and roses on the table. Beautiful food and vintage wines. Sitting opposite each other, gazing at each other, drinking each other in, the air rich with anticipation…

For a few brief, stolen moments—stolen from the sordid reality which was the truth about Alexei Constantin—Eve let herself drift into the bliss of imagining what might have been.

We'd dine together, our eyes entwining, while slowly he would make love to me with his eyes across the table, across the wine, and then, when the meal was finished, he'd rise and take me by the hand, and lead me away to paradise itself, in his arms…his bed…

'Wine, madam?'

The voice of the waiter dissolved her fantasy. She blinked, and realised she must have nodded as well, for the waiter had started to pour pale golden Chardonnay into her glass. Across the table, she could see Alexei Constantin giving his damask napkin a quick flick to spread it out over his lap. Then the waiter was filling his glass as well.

She watched as he lifted the full glass.

'What shall we drink to?' His voice was still smooth, still urbane, and the accent in it did things to Eve's toes.

Again she had to remind herself of the knowledge she had of the sordid side of his character. She gave a prim, constrained smile, the barest she could get away with, as she lifted her own glass.

'A successful outcome to my request to repurchase Beaumont, Mr Constantin,' she said, and took a sip of the chilled vintage wine.

A frown creased across his brow.

'Mr Constantin? I think we know each other better than that, don't you?'

There was a look in his eye, half-glint, half-guarded. Something turned slowly over in Eve's stomach.

She lowered her glass again to the table. She had to stop this, right now.

She blanked her expression. Schooling it as her mother had taught her to do when someone made a social *faux pas* which had to be ignored for the sake of politeness.

'Do we?' she countered. 'I don't think we do, Mr Constantin.'

It was deliberate, quite deliberate. All through that excruciating meal on her father's yacht she had doggedly, deliberately refused to acknowledge—either to herself or to him—that their brief, illusory *prelude* on the terrace by the sea had ever taken place. And she would not acknowledge it now.

Nothing showed in his expression at her snub.

'Then perhaps we should remedy that, *non?*' Alexei spoke the last word in French.

It was as deliberate as her remark to him had been. He wanted to evoke that extraordinary encounter when they had first set eyes on each other, when he had not known who she was—had had no suspicion that she might not be what his whole being was telling him—when out of nowhere a woman had appeared in his life he'd wanted to follow, and kiss, and hold, very, very close to him…

His eyes rested on her now. And as they did so he felt words form in his mind. Carrying in them so much—hope and desire intermingled.

Be who I want you to be—be that woman! Be her! Don't let her have been a mirage, an illusion! I would give anything—everything!—for you to be the woman I want you to be…

The staff started to serve the meal—taking, it seemed to him, an age to do so. But at last it was done, and they whisked away, ready to be summoned back when the next course was required.

Alexei watched Eve start to eat the terrine of smoked trout and rocket. She was still wearing exactly what she'd had on when she'd come to his office. Was it deliberate? Still downplaying her beauty? Was it simply because she hadn't brought any other clothes with her? Or merely that she hadn't bothered to change for the evening?

As ever, he could not tell. Frustration bit through him. He could tell nothing about Eve Hawkwood! Neither her reason for turning up in an outfit that muffled her stunning beauty, nor whether or not she used that same beauty as corruptly as her father had used his wealth.

Well, tonight he would find out. He would find out the truth about Eve Hawkwood—once and for all.

Starting right now.

He spoke again, going straight to the heart of his tormenting uncertainty.

'Why did you run from me that night in the hotel gardens?' There was an intensity in his voice he had not intended, but could not veil.

A little gasp escaped Eve, and he saw her eyes flare. Something surged inside him, primitive and triumphant. Then the flare was gone, the layer of English upper-class social poise fastened back down again under its flawless, unruffled surface.

'I'm afraid moonlight does rather ridiculous things to common sense—especially foreign moonlight,' she answered with a dismissive little smile. Her English accent, she could hear, rang more crystal-cut than ever. She sounded like something out of a Noel Coward play, she knew, but she didn't care. Immediately—the way her mother had taught her to do in such situations, whenever someone made an embarrassing remark—she changed the subject.

'I don't know the Arlington, but I believe it's one of the oldest hotels in London?'

A bright, enquiring look was painted on to her face.

'I have no idea,' said Alexei flatly. His mouth tightened. She was refusing to acknowledge what had happened between them again. But why? The question formed stark and uncomfortable in his mind.

Was it because it had meant nothing to her? Nothing at all? Just another sexual game of Giles Hawkwood's daughter? *Then why isn't she playing on that encounter, your obvious attraction to her? If she is what you fear her to be, she should be playing it for all it's worth! But she isn't—she's stonewalling you on it. Changing the subject...*

Emotion surged through him. Relief—it *was* relief, he knew it. Her reaction just now to his reminder of their first encounter had to be a sign—it had to be!—that his fears about her were unfounded. If Eve Hawkwood were her father's daughter, then wanting something from him, as she did now, she'd have been eager to capitalise all she could on what she must have realised instantly was his attraction to her...his vulnerability to her...

Instead she'd stonewalled him and changed the subject to something totally innocent. He watched her covertly as he started to eat. She did not seem put out by his terse response, and was now talking animatedly about the history of London's famous hotels. He let her continue, paying no attention to whatever she was saying about the Savoy's connection with the operettas of Gilbert and Sullivan, or the Ritz's popularity in the Edwardian period.

Instead he felt his emotions running like a wild river in flood, twisting around in eddies and whirlpools, trying to find a direction to flow in. A true direction—one he could trust and know that he could trust.

But how to find it?

He needed to probe again. Probe into Eve Hawkwood to see if he could find her metal. Base—or precious. He had to know. Whatever it took, he had to know.

He watched while she took another sip of Chardonnay as the waiting staff returned to dispose of the finished first course and serve the entrée, leaving, at his behest, the dessert, coffee and liqueurs on the sideboard, so they need not return again. He did not want any more interruptions.

Not now. Not when he intended, once and for all, to discover who the real Eve Hawkwood was.

Not that he was any closer yet. As she started to cut into her fillet of lamb, the topic of her conversation moved on, like a continuously flowing shallow stream, to how so many of the aristocratic townhouses, such as Grosvenor House, had been demolished after the first World War, to make way for modern hotels. Her expression revealed nothing. For a moment frustration filled him with an intensity that made his breath catch. Damn these ridiculously unreadable upper-class Englishwomen! It was all surface—smooth, unreadable surface—concealing whatever was going on beneath that cool, composed, socially immaculate display, making oh-so-polite conversation.

On an impulse spearing up through him with a sharpness that edged through his voice, he waited until she had paused to take a sip from her wine, then spoke.

'Tell me something—was it a surprise to you that your father lost his company?'

Did anything show in her eyes at his abrupt, pointed question? If it did, it was masked immediately. Her voice, when she answered him, was cool, unfazed either by the abruptness of the question, interrupting her ceaseless flow of banal conversation, or its questionability.

'Yes, it was,' she answered evenly. 'He wasn't a man who looked likely to be defeated.'

'He fought hard,' said Alexei Constantin. His voice was dry.

'I imagine he did,' she answered. Her voice was even drier.

'And used every available weapon.'

Eve felt her nerves tighten. The question had come out of the blue, while her mind had been running in quiet desperation on just how on earth she was going to keep going with a one-sided conversation whose blandness was the only way to keep going through this excruciating ordeal.

Why on earth had he suddenly thrown that at her? She tried to make her tense, tired mind focus. Why was Alexei Constantin talking to her about the success of his takeover of Hawkwood Enterprises? Did he think it had anything to do with her, or why she was here, wanting to buy back Beaumont? And why make that remark about her father using every available weapon? Had there been something in his voice when he'd said that? Why ask her, anyway, and what did he expect her to say, in the circumstances? she thought grimly. That her father was a brutal thug, in business and in life, who wouldn't flinch at fighting dirty, whether it was against the man trying to take his company away from him, or if it was his own wife he took his fist to? She might have no loyalty to her father, and he deserved none, but she was hardly going to expound on his deficiencies to a stranger—even one who'd been locked in bitter corporate struggle with him.

Well, it didn't matter—nothing mattered except getting through this evening.

To that end, she simply replied, her voice still cool, 'I imagine that's standard practice in these matters.'

'That depends,' he said—and there was definitely something in his voice now, 'on whose standards are being applied.'

Eve reached for her wine. She needed it. What on earth was the point of baiting her like this? He couldn't just be making conversation until he decided it was time to tell her whether he was going to sell Beaumont to her. Was he getting some kind of perverse kick out of rubbing in the fact that he'd defeated her father?

Well, what if he was? It was nothing to do with her. Her only reason for being here was to buy back Beaumont. Alexei Constantin was nothing more to her than the man she *had* to convince to sell it back to her.

Had to…

Around her forehead she could feel a band of tension forming. What on earth was the point of this dinner? Why couldn't the man just get on with it and tell her whether or not he was going to sell to her? That was the only reason she was here. The sooner she knew, the sooner she could go—get out of here, away from Alexei Constantin. The band around her forehead tightened. She reached for her wine and took a larger mouthful than usual. As the wine slipped down her throat, she felt its effect. It should have helped calm her overstrung nerves, but instead it seemed to be bringing the room into super-focus.

Bringing Alexei Constantin into super-focus.

She couldn't help it—as she lowered her glass again her eyes went to him. Went to him and she felt the electric jolt go through her, as it had the first time she'd seen him.

Dear God, but she could just gaze at him for ever—

Soaking in every detail—the way his long lashes swept over those dark, assessing eyes, set above those high, knife-cut cheekbones. The way his sable hair crisped at his gleaming white collar. The way his sculpted mouth curved at the edges, the lines from his nose incising into the olive tanned skin of his face. The way his long, lean fingers curled around his wine glass…

He started to speak again, and she forced herself to pay attention. What Alexei Constantin looked like, the fact that he could draw her eyes to him as if he were a magnet and she a helpless compass needle seeking its home, was an irrelevance. She had to remember that. She *must* remember that!

She focussed on listening to his words, but as she did she found them bewildering.

'What standards would *you* apply to business, Miss Hawkwood?'

Eve stared. Why was he harping on about this? She had nothing to do with Hawkwood Enterprises. But he'd asked a question, and social convention required that she give a civil answer. Her years of training gave her no alternative.

'I'm afraid I'm not a businesswoman, Mr Constantin,' she replied, her tone light and inconsequential, masking the emotion swirling beneath the surface.

'No?' Alexei Constantin sat back. 'Yet you are intending to make a substantial purchase, are you not, this evening?'

She raised her eyebrows as she started to go through the motions of addressing the contents of her plate. 'I would hardly call that business,' she answered obliquely.

'The clinic at Beaumont is not a business?' There was irony in his voice. And more than irony—an edge that skittered along her nerves.

But nerves were a luxury she could not indulge.

'No,' she returned steadily. 'It isn't required to show a profit. In the circumstances, it would be hard for it to do so.'

She didn't want to discuss the clinic. She just wanted this meal to be over and Alexei Constantin to agree to the sale of Beaumont. Her nerves were stretched like wire through her body. Instinctively, she reached for her glass of wine again. It seemed to be full. Had Alexei refilled it? How much had she drunk? She couldn't tell. Well, it didn't matter. She took another mouthful, and set the glass down again.

Her mind felt fuzzy, and she didn't want that. She needed it to be sharp—sharp and focussed—focussed on the reason she was here—the only reason she was here. Which was not what she kept finding herself doing…letting her eyes slip across the table towards the man sitting there, drawing her gaze like a magnet.

Desperately, calling on all the long years of training at her mother's side, she cast about for something to say. Anything.

'I noticed that your offices have a blue plaque—commemorating a minor Victorian poet, I believe. They're quite fascinating, the blue plaques in London.'

She was off again, taking refuge in yet more banality. Even to her own ears it sounded tedious. But it was essential she keep speaking. Essential. As she droned on about everything and anything she knew about London's blue plaques, mentioning every one she'd ever seen, however minor the historical personage or event they celebrated, she felt the steel band around her forehead biting into her. Only one thing seemed to loosen it— the continual sips of wine that she was taking to make the food that tasted increasingly like cardboard go down her throat.

Oh, God, when will this ordeal be over? When will he just tell me whether he's going to sell me Beaumont? When can I escape? Please, please, when can I escape…?

The plea went unanswered, though it went round and round and round in her head as she kept the excruciating conversation going the way she was trained to do, allowing no awkward silences to occur.

By the time the endless meal finally drew to a close she was weak with mental exhaustion.

As Alexei Constantin handed her her coffee, taking one for himself, plus a liqueur, which she refused, her nerves tautened even more. Surely to God Alexei Constantin would now put her out of her misery and tell her his intention? She couldn't stand much more of this, she just couldn't.

She *had* to find out. Now. Throwing caution to the winds, she replaced the cream jug and said, keeping her voice as light and socially polite as ever, 'So, may I ask if you've made your decision yet, Mr Constantin, over selling Beaumont?'

She looked enquiringly across the table. Her expression was bland, neutral. She must not let it be anything else. But inside she could feel her nerves stretching, like a piece of elastic with a lead weight dragging it down to breaking point. He was looking back at her. There was a focus in his eyes that tightened like wire around her throat. Yet his gaze had no expression in it. None at all.

And that, suddenly, chilled her like a trickle of ice down her spine.

Then, leaning back in his chair as he picked up his cognac glass and swirled its dark golden contents contemplatively, he spoke.

'Tell me,' he said, and his voice sounded more accented than she had ever heard it, 'how badly do you want to recover this property?'

Eve felt her stomach lurch. Oh, God, was he trying to up the price he was going to demand? Had she been stupid simply to offer him the market price straight away? Well, too late to repine now. Instead, she fortified herself with another sip of wine.

'Mr Constantin,' she began, 'the valuation I've given you is a fair market one—I am not trying to buy back Beaumont on the cheap.'

She left it at that. She had no intention of discussing her dire financial affairs with this man.

For a moment he kept his gaze levelled on her.

Eve Hawkwood clearly had no need to skimp on the price for what she wanted. No need to worry about spending several million pounds to get this property back. Not that he was surprised—whether or not Giles Hawkwood was ruined or not, his wife and daughter would have financial resources of their own. Their class always did. There would be trust funds and share portfolios, property and other assets to draw on, and a network of wealthy friends and relations to help them keep their lives luxurious and idle.

His mouth twisted momentarily. Anyone who simply wanted to own again a clinic they frequented for their own personal use could certainly not be constrained financially. Owning your own rehab clinic must surely rank as one of the luxuries of life.

Compunction pricked at him briefly. Marriage to Giles Hawkwood would have given any woman cause to turn to alcohol, or worse.

Ruthlessly, he put aside his compunction. He was not concerned with Giles Hawkwood's wife.

Only with his daughter.

To discover, finally, what she was. Long dark lashes swept momentarily down over Alexei's eyes, veiling them.

Under her ribs, Eve felt her heart begin to thump. This was the moment of truth—would he sell or not? She had nothing more to offer. Nothing at all.

For a moment he did not reply, and she could feel her tension mount unbearably.

Then, at last, his eyes lifted to hers again. Their expression was still completely unreadable. Absently he swirled the cognac in his glass again. She wanted to look at it, to watch the movement of the rich, fragrant liquor, wanted to tear her eyes away from him and look anywhere else but at him, be anywhere else but here. She found she was holding her breath.

'Money,' said Alexei Constantin, and his gaze rested on her, shuttered, expressionless, 'is not the only currency. What else can you offer to persuade me to sell to you?'

His voice was quite expressionless, the gaze resting on her likewise. And yet there was something in them that prickled across her skin.

She looked at him.

'I'm afraid I don't understand.'

Her voice sounded more clipped than ever, almost a caricature of an upper-class accent. But it was the only way she could hang on to the rigid self-control she needed now, when her nerves were snapping with tension.

Slowly he took a mouthful of cognac, then set down his glass, keeping his hand curved around the bowl. He was leaning back in his chair, his white shirt pulled taut across his chest, his dark jacket emphasising the leanness of his body. She tried not to look, tried to keep her self-control in place. But it was hopeless, useless. Awareness of him flooded through her. Awareness of his physique, his body, his overpowering presence across the table from her.

It was the curve of his fingers around the cognac glass, cupping its base, his short, white-rimmed nails edging the glass. It was the column of his throat and the white of his collar, the long dark slash of his tie and the taut expanse of his shirt across his torso beneath. It was the lean strength of his body as he leant back in his chair, the slight tilt of his head as his gaze rested on her with the veiled, expressionless regard in those powerful, dark eyes that seemed to be able to see through her. It was the high cut of his cheekbones, the straight slash of his nose, the lines edging his mouth…

I can't stop it… The awareness of her own helplessness, her own complete inability to get her body, her mind, back under control, was floating somewhere, but she could not seize it. She could only just go on doing what she was doing now, feeling the wine she had so foolishly let herself drink winding in her veins, weakening her fatally, the ever increasing tension finally overcoming her…

I can't stop it…

Even as she gazed across at him she could feel the pulse of her veins at her wrists, her throat—and in her body, quickening through her. She tried to stop it, quench it, but she could not. She was helpless—helpless to do anything at all except go on doing what she was doing.

Her eyes were dilating; she knew it. She could see his face going slightly, very slightly, out of focus. She tried to bring him back into focus, but she couldn't do that either. Her breathing seemed shallower, her lungs lacking oxygen. There was a thickness in them, in her veins, in the air around her.

He was getting to his feet. She didn't know why. Did it mean he wanted her to go? That he wasn't going to accept her offer even though it was all she had? Her eyes followed him helplessly as he moved around the table. Then he was standing behind her chair. Was he waiting for her to stand up? So that she would go, clear out, stop annoying him with requests to buy back a property he had no interest in, which meant nothing to him and yet to her meant so much?

Oh, God, if he were really throwing her out, refusing her offer, she couldn't, *couldn't* just give in like this!

'What did you mean—money is not the only currency?'

Her voice was husked. She didn't mean it to be, but she couldn't help it. Her voice seemed not to be working properly. She wanted to get to her feet, but she couldn't. She wanted to twist her head round and back, so that she could look at him when she spoke to him, but she couldn't do that either. She could only hold still. Very, very still. Waiting, while everything thickened around her, for him to explain. Wild thoughts bucketed through her. None made sense. None at all.

'Do you really...' his voice was different somehow, lower-pitched, and more than that, but she didn't know what it was '...need that spelled out?'

And as he spoke, his hand slid caressingly across the nape of her neck.

He felt her quiver. Felt the tremor of her flesh as he stroked that most sensitive part of a woman's body, that subtle erogenous zone, so innocuous and yet so potent, that could stimulate an onset of arousal in the whole body.

She didn't move. Just went on sitting there, looking at the place across the table where he had been. He could not see her face, but he did not need to. The message she had given to him so bountifully, so unambiguously, as she'd given her reaction to his opening bid, had told him what he'd needed to know. That the moment he'd given his first indication that the price for what she wanted might be more than financial she had responded accordingly. He had watched her drop her careful, cultivated pose of indifference to him, seen it dissolve before his eyes, to be replaced by something quite different. Gone, absolutely, was the cool, classic upper-class English beauty who made polite, insipid conversation over the dinner table whatever the circumstances—whether it was her lout of a father interjecting his coarse comments, or himself stonewalling her as he had all through the meal, to see if she would persevere with her role, as indeed, she had, doggedly, to the very end.

But that had gone the moment he'd made it clear that it was not what he required. That what was required was something quite different.

And she'd responded immediately.

Unambiguously. Because no man could possibly mistake the message that had come from her just now, loud and clear.

Just as no man could mistake the reaction she was giving him now, as he moved in to touch her physically.

Eve Hawkwood was sexually available to him.

And she was signalling it on all frequencies.

He stepped back.

'Get up.' He spoke softly, but there was command in his voice. He watched as she obeyed it. Well, he thought, she would, wouldn't she? She would do anything he told her to. Anything that would be to her advantage.

Emotion was cutting through him. He didn't know what it was, but it sliced like the sharpest blade. He ignored it. It was irrelevant.

All that was relevant was that Eve Hawkwood was proving to be what he had thought her. He had put her to the test and she had shown her true nature. The mask had come off—that cool, immaculate mask of well-bred aristocratic daughter of well-bred aristocratic mother. Revealing, beneath, what she truly was. Her father's daughter. Ready to trade in any currency required to achieve her ends.

Ready to trade her beautiful, desirable body to get what she wanted.

The emotion he could not name and did not want to cut through him again, powerful and insistent. A voice was speaking inside his head. He wanted to ignore it, but it was demanding to be heard.

This isn't proof! This shows nothing—nothing at all! Nothing except that Eve Hawkwood lights up for you! That isn't evidence to condemn her—

He cut through the voice, silencing it. Even as he did so Eve Hawkwood had risen and turned to face him. The emotion he was trying to crush scythed through him again, as if cutting him off at the knees. Her eyes were wide, distended. Her mouth was parted, trembling.

He wanted, God, how he wanted to reach for her, to mould her to him, shape her body to his, open her mouth with his, taste her honey.

As he had tasted it once before, in those brief, out-of-time, out-of-reality moments when moonlight had suffused her like a dream, a fantasy.

He felt his hand reach out. Felt his thumb brush against the rich, velvet swell of her lips. Then slowly, infinitely slowly, he lowered his head to hers.

It was bliss. His mouth was like silk. The taste of cognac was on his lips, his tongue, as she unresistingly opened her mouth to his. She let him ease his silken tongue to hers, let his mouth move on hers, let his hand slide to cup the base of her head, holding her for him while he deepened his kiss, while he took his long, leisurely fill of her.

Her weakness was absolute. Since the moment he had touched her, stroking the ultra-sensitive nape of her neck, she had been helpless and boneless, incapable of anything, any last vestige of rational thought. It had all dissolved away, melted away. She could not have said where she was, or why—only that she was trembling in every limb, every cell of her body.

Somewhere deep inside her, so deep it was buried, suffocated, was a voice telling her she was mad, insane, that she must not let this happen, that all she wanted of Alexei Constantin was his agreement to sell Beaumont, that it was insanity to let *him* kiss her like this—a man to whom women were nothing more than sexual commodities to be enjoyed for cash.

He wasn't the man she'd thought him, the fantasy she'd yearned for.

But now, in this exquisite drowning of sensations, he was— he was that fantasy, remembered, relived, reclaimed.

She felt all the tension that had been racing through her, twisting tighter and tighter around her, all evening, all day, all the weeks, months, *years* of her life, simply dissolve away in one endless wave of bliss.

Gone, all gone. Miraculously, blissfully. And she gave herself to it, completely and without reservation. Ardently. Absolutely.

And then the kiss ended.

He was drawing back from her, putting her aside from him. She swayed, bereft of strength, gazing at him helplessly.

He took a step back. His face was like a mask. But there was something in his eyes, something that shot through her. She didn't know what it was, but it made her spine suddenly chill, like ice.

He walked to the table and picked up his cognac glass. He took a mouthful, then placed it back on the white tablecloth. He looked across at her. His face was still like a mask, but now his eyes were shuttered as well. Whatever had been in them had gone. Eve stared at him. She couldn't do anything else. Her blood was pulsing in her body, her limbs weak and boneless. Without realising it she closed her hand over the back of her chair, as if to gain strength from it. Her mind was in turmoil, her senses overloaded, still resonating with his touch.

For one long, silent moment Alexei Constantin simply looked at her. Then he spoke.

An Important Message from the Editors

Dear Reader,

Because you've chosen to read one of our fine romance novels, we'd like to say "thank you!" And, as a **special** way to thank you, we've selected <u>two more</u> of the books you love so well **plus** two exciting Mystery Gifts to send you — absolutely <u>FREE</u>!

Please enjoy them with our compliments...

Pam Powers

Lift here

Peel off seal and place inside...

How to validate your Editor's "Thank You" FREE GIFTS

1. Peel off gift seal from front cover. Place it in space provided at right. This automatically entitles you to receive 2 FREE BOOKS and 2 FREE mystery gifts.

2. Send back this card and you'll get 2 new Harlequin *Presents®* novels. These books have a cover price of $4.50 or more each in the U.S. and $5.25 or more each in Canada, but they are yours to keep absolutely free.

3. There's no catch. You're under no obligation to buy anything. We charge nothing—ZERO—for your first shipment. And you don't have to make any minimum number of purchases— not even one!

4. The fact is, thousands of readers enjoy receiving their books by mail from The Harlequin Reader Service®. They enjoy the convenience of home delivery...they like getting the best new novels at discount prices BEFORE they're available in stores... and they love their Reader to Reader subscriber newsletter featuring author news, special book offers, book reviews and much more!

5. We hope that after receiving your free books you'll want to remain a subscriber. But the choice is yours— to continue or cancel, any time at all! So why not take us up on our invitation, with no risk of any kind. You'll be glad you did!

GET TWO *Free* MYSTERY GIFTS...

SURPRISE MYSTERY GIFTS COULD BE YOURS **FREE** AS A SPECIAL "THANK YOU" FROM THE EDITORS

The Editor's "Thank You" Free Gifts Include:

- Two NEW Romance novels!
- Two exciting mystery gifts!

Yes! I have placed my
Editor's "Thank You" seal in the
space provided at right. Please
send me 2 free books and
2 free mystery gifts. I
understand I am under no
obligation to purchase any
books, as explained on the
back and on the opposite page.

PLACE
FREE GIFTS
SEAL
HERE

306 HDL EFZ3   **106 HDL EFYS**

FIRST NAME

LAST NAME

ADDRESS

APT.#

CITY

STATE/PROV.

ZIP/POSTAL CODE

(H-P-10/06)

Thank You!

The Harlequin Reader Service® — Here's How It Works:

Accepting your 2 free books and 2 free mystery gifts places you under no obligation to buy anything. You may keep the books and gifts and return the shipping statement marked "cancel." If you do not cancel, about a month later we'll send you 6 additional books and bill you just $3.80 each in the U.S., or $4.47 each in Canada, plus 25¢ shipping & handling per book and applicable taxes if any.* That's the complete price and — compared to cover prices starting from $4.50 each in the U.S. and $5.25 each in Canada — it's quite a bargain! You may cancel at any time, but if you choose to continue, every month we'll send you 6 more books, which you may either purchase at the discount price or return to us and cancel your subscription.

*Terms and prices subject to change without notice. Sales tax applicable in N.Y. Canadian residents will be charged applicable provincial taxes and GST. All orders subject to approval. Credit or debit balances in a customer's account(s) may be offset by any other outstanding balance owed by or to the customer. Please allow 4 to 6 weeks for delivery.

BUSINESS REPLY MAIL

FIRST-CLASS MAIL   PERMIT NO. 717-003   BUFFALO, NY

POSTAGE WILL BE PAID BY ADDRESSEE

HARLEQUIN READER SERVICE
3010 WALDEN AVE
PO BOX 1867
BUFFALO NY 14240-9952

NO POSTAGE
NECESSARY
IF MAILED
IN THE
UNITED STATES

'I'll accept the price you offer on one condition. You spend the night with me.'

She heard the words, but they did not make sense. It was as if they were in a foreign language that she did not speak.

'Do you accept the condition?'

There was no emotion in his voice. That was what she registered first. Then, slowly, the sense of what he had said resolved in her brain.

It was like walking head-first into a brick wall at speed.

She heard her own breath draw in sharply. Saw his expression change fractionally. Then he was speaking again.

'You are doubtless used to a less overt proposition in such situations, but I have no time for that. This is a very simple deal. You pay me the market price, at the valuation you've presented me with, plus you spend the night with me. Is there a problem?'

Something was happening to her, Eve knew. She was imploding. Very slowly.

He'd kissed her. He'd kissed her and melted her bones. Taken her, for a few timeless moments, back into that fleeting fantasy, making it blissfully, magically real again.

But it hadn't been real. It had been as false as it had been last time.

He was speaking again, and she heard the words. But she could only stand there, blank, disbelieving.

'You're looking affronted. What did you expect? Moonlight and stars, romance and sweet nothings, as it was in France? That was then, Eve—*this,* this is now.'

There was a sardonic note in his voice. Mocking.

It was like a knife sliding in between her ribs. Painless, but mortal. She went on standing there, completely frozen. She couldn't move.

Her immobility seemed to irritate him.

'Eve, this is very straightforward. I really can't make it any clearer to you. It's your decision. It doesn't matter to me one way or the other if I sell Beaumont to you, or to anyone else, or don't sell it at all. You're the one who wants to buy it.' He started to walk towards the door. 'I'm going to bed. Either join me there, or go home.'

She watched him walk out of the suite's dining room, heard the door to the bedroom across the entrance hallway open, then close again.

Then there was silence.

Silence everywhere except in her head, where there was a voice. A voice saying over and over again, *I don't believe this. I don't believe this. I don't believe this...*

CHAPTER SEVEN

ALEXEI stood by the window of his bedroom, hands sunk deep in his trouser pockets, looking down at the London street below. The traffic was light, only a few cars and taxis sweeping by, and few pedestrians.

He saw none of it.

Eve Hawkwood was about to reveal the truth about herself. Now, finally, he would know the truth about her. A truth as unambiguous as the test he'd set her. Deliberately he'd put the choice in front of her in the starkest terms—terms she could not possibly dress up as anything other than the base, sordid offer that it was. And what she did about it would show him the truth about her. Either she would storm out in fury—repulsed by what he had demanded of her—or she would not.

And if she did not—

His hands clenched.

If she did not storm out, then he would know that he had been right. That she was nothing but her father's creature. Using her body to get what she wanted.

Corrupt. Soiled. Worthless.

Untouchable.

The grim tightening of his mouth as the word formed in his

mind had no humour in it. If Eve Hawkwood failed the test he was setting her then she would be untouchable indeed.

He would not soil his hands on her.

Eve stood quite motionless. There was not a sound to be heard, except the muffled noise from the traffic outside. All around her was complete stillness.

Yet in the bedroom close by Alexei Constantin was waiting for her to go to him and have sex with him.

Sex on terms that were, for him, perfectly normal…perfectly acceptable.

Perfectly familiar.

An image resolved in her brain. Alexei Constantin walking out of the nightclub in the Côte d'Azur with a prostitute on his arm, taking her back to his room to pay for sex with her.

Words formed in her mind, falling like stones. This time the payment would not be cash, but the title deeds to Beaumont.

What did you expect? Moonlight and stars, romance and sweet nothings?

The mockery slayed her. Ground into dust even the memory of those few wonderful moments. The bliss she had felt just now, as he had kissed her, had brought that memory searingly to life again. A memory she'd nailed down so tight it had had no room to breathe, no room to exist.

But it had got free.

Dismay hollowed out inside her.

It was me—I let it out. She had let him see, in her face, her eyes, what he could do to her, how her stupid, treacherous, be-traying body reacted to him.

Dismay flooded her, along with guilt and self-accusation. Oh, God, she'd opened herself up for this! She'd signalled to him and he had homed straight in on it!

And now he wanted to collect. Collect on the terms he was accustomed to offering to those women he used for sex.

The nausea went through her again. And another wave of disbelief.

She shut her eyes, trying to shut out what was happening to her. But it wasn't any good. She was here, in a private suite, and Alexei Constantin had just informed her, coolly and indifferently, that he expected sex with her if she wanted him to agree to sell her back Beaumont.

Beaumont. The reason she was here. The only reason. To get Beaumont back.

And she *would* get Beaumont back.

She must get Beaumont back, whatever it cost her.

In her eyes was a bleakness she would have given anything not to have there.

This is what he's like. You knew it—you knew it the moment Pierre told you that woman was a prostitute!

Yes, she had known it—but up until this moment she had never understood, never felt, just how hideous that truth about Alexei Constantin was to her.

You wanted him to be someone different.

But he wasn't. He was what she had known him to be since her illusions about him had been ripped away. And the pain cut through her like a knife through living flesh.

No! It doesn't matter! It didn't matter then, and it doesn't matter now. All that matters now is what are you going to do?

The bleakness in her eyes leached into her face.

She had to get Beaumont back for her mother—for all who depended on it.

That was all there was to it. No other option. No other choice.

I have to do this. The words dropped like stones in her head. *I cannot not do this. Because if I don't, I couldn't live with myself.*

Too late she heard another voice in her head—*Can you live with yourself if you do?*

She pushed it aside. She must not listen to it. It was an irrelevance. Out of nowhere, a blow had fallen that she had never expected. It had come out of the blue, and she was still paralysed with disbelief. But it was a disbelief she could not afford.

This is real—real. He means it—he really means it. He wants me to have sex with him, or he won't sell me Beaumont.

Her throat constricted. Bitter with gall.

Has it really come to this after all? What my father wanted of me all along? My God, how he would laugh—coarse and scathing and satisfied that I've finally been reduced to doing what he always wanted me to do…

Her eyes shifted, memory forcing its way through the years. She'd been eighteen when her father had come into her bedroom while she was dressing for a business dinner party he'd summoned her to. He'd looked her over, told her to leave her hair loose, and informed her that one of the guests that night had an eye for young girls.

'I want him kept sweet,' he'd told her brusquely. 'And I don't care what it takes you to do that. Do you understand me? You do whatever it takes. The contract I want from him is worth a lot of money to me.'

She'd looked right back at him.

'Don't *ever*,' she'd said, her voice frigid, 'say *anything* like that to me again. *I* know what you are, but you really, *really* don't want the tabloids knowing it too—do you? And don't think I wouldn't. My God, they'd have a field-day if they knew about the home life of Giles Hawkwood! Even *you* wouldn't be able to shut them all up—the proprietor of the *Globe* hates your guts ever since you slept with his wife. He'd kill to get the goods on you!'

It had been touch and go, and she had been shaking with fear as well as fury, but her defiance—something he was not used to in his dealings with others—had worked. Her father had backed off, making do with merely having her look decorative and well-bred. But there'd been a victim of her dangerous defiance that night all the same.

Her mother had appeared the next morning with a particularly heavy covering of foundation and powder.

Her mother…

Eve's throat constricted again.

Resolution steeled through her. What the hell did it matter? One night of sex with Alexei Constantin. She could bear it—she *must* bear it. If it was prostitution, then the guilt was his, not hers.

But her mother would not suffer one more moment of the pain and anguish she had suffered all her married life, all through the hell of being Mrs Giles Hawkwood.

This ends now. I will not—will not—let my mother go through any more. She's got to have Beaumont—it's the only thing that keeps her going. I've got to get it back for her. I've just got to. She needs Beaumont.

And not just her mother.

So many others needed Beaumont.

She saw it now, in her mind's vision. Bathed in sunlight, its warm red brick aged by centuries, nestled into the woodlands of the sheltering fold of the hills in which it stood, its grounds and gardens stretching down to the fields in the valley below. A beautiful, gracious house.

And more, so much more than a mere house. A refuge from a harsh world, a sanctuary, a safe, protecting place.

For all whom it sheltered.

And the only way she could get it back was to have sex with Alexei Constantin. There was no other way. He had made that crystal-clear—brutally clear. As she said the words to herself, something so powerful rose in her that she thought she must shatter into a thousand pieces. It buckled outwards like an explosion underground. For a moment she thought it would rip her apart.

Then, with superhuman effort, she hammered it back down. Crushed it, forced it down, nailing it down so tight that it almost hurt her. Then, over the surface, she slid something so familiar, so close-fitting that it was a second skin. She had worn it for years—all her life.

She would wear it still.

And it would get her through. Get her through what she had to get through. Just as it had got her through everything else in her life.

I can do this. Because if I don't do this I will never, ever forgive myself. It's got to be done. It's just got to be done. And that is all there is to it. It's not my fault, not my responsibility. Not my guilt. And I can do it. I must do it—

Slowly, deliberately, she opened her eyes again.

Slowly, deliberately, she walked to the door.

Alexei stood under the shower, hot water pounding down over him. His nerves were as tight as wire stretched to breaking point. Waiting to see what Eve Hawkwood would prove to be was unbearable, and on an impulse he had headed for the bathroom, for something—anything—to do. Now, as the needles of water drummed into his shoulders, his back, as he leant, hands resting on the slippery tiles, head bowed, he found words circling endlessly in his head.

Don't let her be there when I come out. Let her have stormed off. Furious and disgusted. Then I can go after her—woo her, start again, undo all that was. Knowing, with clear, incontrovertible proof, that she was—is—the woman I want her to be. Dear God—let her be the woman I want her to be…

All evening that hope had been there, but he had kept it silent, as silent as he could, as he got through that interminable meal, with rigid self-control imposed across every synapse in his brain.

There had been only one moment when he'd let that control slip.

One single, explosive, potent moment.

Hell, he should never have let himself kiss her like that! Never let himself feel the velvet softness of her mouth, seeking and finding the honeyed nectar within.

He'd been insane to let himself touch her, taste her. Torture to let her go, to make her that despicable offer that he was now praying with all his strength she would fling back in his face with outrage and contempt.

Don't let her be there when I come out.

Emotion twisted through him, hard and unbearable. With a sudden jerk he levered himself upright, cut off the water, and stepped out of the shower, patting his body with a large white bathtowel and drying himself briefly before wrapping it around his hips.

There was no noise from the bedroom beyond.

Face expressionless, he opened the bathroom door.

Don't let her be there.

She was there.

Something shot through him, a killing blow. He could feel it impacting, as if in slow motion, emptying through his guts.

So now he knew. He had his answer. Written in letters ten feet high. The answer he would have given everything not to have.

He stood for a moment, his hand splayed against the doorjamb, his body so tense it could have been made out of steel, feeling the killing blow reverberate through him, body and soul.

Then, along with the disappointment buckling through him, another sensation began to gather.

She had her back to him, her glorious hair loosened, cascading over her shoulders, and she was taking her clothes off. Very neatly, very methodically. Already her suit jacket and skirt were draped over a chair in the bedroom, her shoes and handbag placed tidily beside it, and now she was taking off her stockings.

He watched, a muscle twitching in his cheek, as with every ounce of his being he hammered rigid, absolute control over his body.

He would not allow it to react to her.

Move—do something! Don't just stand and watch—

But he could not move. Not a muscle.

Her hands slid down her legs, each foot resting in turn on the chair as she removed each silky sliver. She then shook each stocking lightly, draped them over the skirt. Then, as he watched, she slipped off her suspender belt and panties and added them to the pile.

He felt beads of sweat start to prick out along his damp spine.

Stop her—stop her now—

Her hands were sliding around her back, unfastening her bra. With a complicated movement she seemed to shrug it off without removing her slip.

He felt heat gather in his loins as she neatly placed the bra over her other underclothes. The tension in his body was agony.

Get rid of her. In God's name—get rid of her! Just—get her out of here!

He jerked his hand away from the doorjamb.

'Nice show, Eve, but you've wasted your time. The deal's off.'

His voice was as cold, as harsh, as death.

Eve stilled.

She'd known he was there, had to be there, because the shower had stopped, and she'd heard the muffled noise of the bathroom door opening.

But she couldn't have turned around to save her life. The numbness in her was absolute. She was like some kind of robot—methodically, soullessly, going through some kind of automatic function.

Removing her clothes so she could go to bed and have sex with

Alexei Constantin. So he would sell Beaumont to her, so her mother could be safe, so that everyone who needed Beaumont could be safe.

The logic was irrefutable. Inescapable.

In the numbness of her brain she heard his words, but they didn't make sense.

Slowly, she turned to face him.

For a moment all she could do was feel the blood leap in her veins as her eyes took in his lean, honed body. He was wearing nothing but a towelling bathrobe, skimming his muscled thighs, revealing the deep vee of his bare, hard chest. She felt her breasts tighten and tauten.

Her blood swirled, misting her eyes.

Then, like a drain opening, it fell back, sucking down into the pit of her stomach, where it met the ice that was gelling through her.

What did he mean—the deal was off?

She stared at him, trying to make the words make sense, but they would not. What did he mean? She had done exactly what he'd told her to do. She'd had to turn into a robot to do it, but she was here, wasn't she? Getting ready to spend the night with him, have sex with him, get Beaumont back in the only way he was allowing her to.

So why say what he had? It didn't make sense.

She saw his face darken as she stared at him.

'Don't look like that—it's simple enough. The deal is off. Now, get your clothes back on and get out. I'm not selling Beaumont to you.'

His voice grated like metal on metal.

Eve stared, her eyes widening.

'*What? What* did you say?'

A nerve ticked in his cheek. She could see it—see the lean curves of his face, the high cut of his cheekbones, the sculpted blade of his nose, his mouth, the sable feathering of his hair, the shuttered darkness of his eyes…

Eyes she could not tear hers from. Eyes she was starting to drown in.

'You heard me. Get dressed and clear out.'

His voice raked her back. Back into the reality of where she was. Why she was there.

The numbness dropped from her. In its place a great wave was billowing up through her. Huge and overpowering.

'You want me to do *what?*' she echoed, disbelieving.

An expression flickered across his face and was gone. 'Don't make an issue of this, Eve. The deal is off. No sale. No discussion. Now, just go.'

She heard only one phrase through the huge wave, through the blurred burning in her veins, her lungs. *No sale.* That was all she heard. No sale. No sale of Beaumont. No buying it back. No restoring it to her mother. No keeping it safe for her, for all those who needed it, relied on it for their refuge, their shelter from an unkind world.

'Why?'

The word stung from her. Demanding an answer. Inside her, she could feel that wave building dangerously. His eyes looked across at her, flickering with emotion, then returning to their veiled and shuttered state.

'I said no discussion. Just put your clothes back on and go.'

The words fell from him like cold, condemning stones.

The wave inside her broke. Emotion poured through her. Hot and angry and drenching. He was starting to turn away. She could see it. She saw it, and reacted to it. Fury boiled through her—through her veins, her body. He'd demanded sex from her as his price for selling Beaumont, and now he was telling he was changing his mind? He'd put her through that hell and now he was saying no sale? Sending her home empty-handed after what he'd demanded of her?

Fury closed over her. Fury and desperation.

She stepped towards him, her hand reaching out to him, catching at his arm. It felt like steel but she didn't care. Didn't care in the least. Alexei Constantin wasn't turning away from her and telling her no sale. Not now, not ever.

Her eyes were glittering. Febrile and focussed—focussed utterly on one thing only. His face. She reached with her other hand, reached for his other arm. Closed her fingers bitingly over the smooth, hard flesh. She closed in on him, her eyes hanging on to his, feeling her hair tumbling over her bare shoulders, feeling the silk of her slip slither over her naked body beneath. She lifted her face to him, her lips parting. She could feel her hair moving over the bare skin of her back. Her hands pressed on his arms, feeling their strength.

He didn't move. Not a muscle. He was completely and absolutely still.

But it was the stillness of absolute tension.

His eyes looked down at her. She could feel them boring through the veil that still shuttered hers, and she could sense the same tension in his gaze as in his whole body.

His cheekbones stood out like etched stone, his mouth tight and compressed.

No sale.

The phrase echoed in her mind. No sale.

Well, Alexei Constantin *was* going to sell to her. He was going to keep to his deal. He wasn't turning on her now, like this, not after what he'd demanded of her! He wasn't going to renege on her—not now! Not when she'd forced herself to come in here, take off her clothes, steel herself to do what even her monster of a father had never got her to do—to have deliberate, cold-blooded sex with a man in order to get something she wanted.

Needed.

Needed desperately. Because there was no other way of

getting it. Because Alexei Constantin was a degenerate, corrupt piece of scum who bought the sex he wanted from women who sold it to him—for a price.

The way she was going to have to force herself to do.

And no way was Alexei Constantin going to cheat her.

Her eyes glittered up at him, like diamonds. Her hands splayed over his arms, her face lifted to his, the hair cascading over her bare shoulders, her breasts swelling beneath the thin, pale silk that was all that covered her. She swayed towards him, the tips of her breasts brushing against the front of his robe. She felt them harden at the touch, felt a quiver go down her spine.

He was looking down at her, his eyes like black pools. Nothing showed in them. No light, no depth. At one white-edged cheekbone a nerve pulsed.

She could see it, visibly, the effort he was exerting, the iron, rigid self-control.

She wanted to break it—shatter it.

But *he* had to do it. *He* had to crack, not her. *She* was the one he'd summoned to his bed—and then rejected.

No sale.

But Alexei Constantin *was* going to sell. He was going to sell. And he was going to break.

Suddenly, violently, his arms jerked, shattering her hold on him, and his hands clamped over her shoulders. His strength was formidable, like iron pressing into her flesh, the tips of his fingers branded her.

She felt the breath leave her body.

For a second, an instant, it hung in the balance. She knew it—could feel it. He would thrust her back.

Her eyes flared. The breath seared in her lungs, lifting her breasts. The tautness of the silk pulled lower, exposing the swell of her breasts, the thrust of her hardened, peaking nipples. For one second longer the hands at her shoulders tensed, as if to push her from him as her eyes seared into his.

Then, with a twist of his features, those hands yanked her forward. Hard against him.

His mouth crushed down on hers.

Triumph surged through Eve. For one glorious, intoxicating, raging moment she felt it—felt the furious, angry, vicious satisfaction of her triumph burn through her. And then it was gone.

Swept away. Swept away by something so powerful it made anything she'd felt till now as insignificant as the bite of a flea against the bite of a tiger.

She was devoured by it.

His mouth crushed against hers; his hands pressed her down—so that she couldn't move, or think, or feel anything except the devouring of her mouth by his. His hands kneaded into her shoulders, twisting into her flesh, pinioning her, possessing her. She was hauled against him, her body hard against his, and her mouth was twisting, her tongue twisting, twining, mating.

She heard a gasp escape her throat. Her hands squeezed over his biceps, glorying in the resistance, because they were like iron—incompressible, rigid. His mouth moved and crushed, lifting and crushing again. The angle of his head changed, lifting and descending again, and she caught his mouth with hers, half-biting, half-yielding. And through her whole body—her breasts, her mouth, her flesh—flared and seared lightning, striking through her—lightning that fed upon itself, fed upon him, on her, hot and violent and burning, burning.

It was instant, it was total. She wanted him—wanted him totally, consumingly. She could feel her hands slip from his arms, slide urgently inside the towelling to smooth across his hard, planed torso. She pressed against him, pressing her body up against his, wanting, aching to feel the hard thrust of his hips against hers, even through the thick barrier of his robe.

And then the robe was gone. How or where she didn't know, didn't care. She was pressing against him, her breasts full, engorged, straining against the silk of her slip, and she wanted to feel them crushed against his torso. So she slid her hands around his back, fingertips pressing hotly into the flex and play of the muscles of his back.

Her arousal was intense. Overpowering. She wanted more—much more. There was another noise in her throat, a quick, urgent panting, and she jerked back her mouth, drawing in great gasps of air into her burning lungs.

He scooped her up. In a single powerful movement he had lifted her, cupping her around her thighs, her shoulders, and then, in the same movement, he had tossed her down on to the bed. The breath was expelled from her lungs, and then he was on her, crushing her down, his hard, heavy body completely covering hers.

Her hips twisted, lifting towards him, wanting him, wanting to feel that hot, hard pressure of his masculinity pressing her down. Excitement shot through her as she felt the force of his own answering arousal. She writhed again, her head tossing from side to side, burning with the urgency of what she wanted.

What she had wanted since the first time her eyes had met his as he walked across the casino floor.

It had electrified her then, and it did so now. Now, when his body was crushing her down, when his left hand was lifting her wrists above her tossing head, keeping her immobile, exposing the rich, ripe aching mounds of her breasts, which his right hand was kneading and shaping, pulling quick, urgent cries gasping from her—now, when his eyes were blazing down into hers, narrowed to slits, with a dark, devouring light in them that was holding her in place for him as surely as the heavy weight of his thighs, the iron lock on her wrists. Now it simply exploded inside her.

She couldn't stop. Not for an instant, a second. Not to clear her mind or be aware of anything except the explosion of sensation detonating through her. It was all she wanted. All she craved. Nothing else existed except this furnace of ravening desire that she was burning in.

His hand left her breast, lifting away from its ripe, swollen mound, and it was a loss that made her almost cry out with frustration as she writhed against him, her wrists straining against the hold on them as if she wanted to seize his hand and press it back in place again, over the aching, throbbing peak. Then, with an incredulous gasp of pleasure, she felt a whole new explosion of sensation detonate. His dark head had lowered to her, and then suddenly, shockingly, his mouth was suckling her, pulling and laving, stroking with his tongue, arousing and stimulating her until she could hardly bear the sheer sensual overload. Her head arched back, exposing her throat, and her short, quick cries raced to a higher pitch. She freed a hand and closed it around his skull, feeling the dark silk of his hair. She kneaded her fingers into his scalp, his nape, as suddenly, abruptly, he changed to the other breast, doing to it what he'd done to its engorged twin. Teeth nipped at her nipple, grazing its pebbled peak in a pleasure so intense she could only gasp, her head pressing back into the pillow, her eyes dilated.

But even as she gave herself to that scorching sensation, there came another piercing sense of loss. His hips had lifted from her, and she gave a cry of protest, instinctively lifting hers upwards, as if to catch him back. But her hips encountered not his hips, but his hand, urgently parting her thighs.

Consumed, burning, her body on fire, aflame with arousal, frenzied with a raw, ravenous hunger for what only he could give her *now,* right now, she lifted to him, straining upwards, the muscles of her thighs taut and pulled, her neck and spine arched, lips parted, eyes dilated and blind—blind to everything except the need, the all-consuming, all-ravening hunger that was driving her, whipping her, devouring her.

For one long, agonising moment he kept her waiting while he guided himself towards her, and then he drove into her—hard and thrusting and filling her totally, absolutely.

She cried out, jerking upwards. Sensation exploded in her. Splintering through her, ripping her apart. He thrust again, driving in harder yet, and harder, and she cried out again, and again. Everywhere, through her whole body, flame was sheeting out, again and again, in hot, pulsing waves that set fire to fire to fire. He drove in one last time, and she strained her hips upwards to the maximum, her thighs and legs and back muscles exerting the maximum pressure to work against him. And as she did so the pressure burst, in a sensation so incredible she could only cry out again—a sharp, high, incredulous note as a pleasure so intense, so unbelievable coursed through her.

It went on, and on, and on, blotting out everything—everything except its own existence. And still it went on.

Her voice was crying out, torn from her throat, her lungs, and then suddenly, abruptly, she hunched forward, jerking inwards, bowing her head, her pinioned wrist contorted against his imprisoning grip, legs convulsing to lift and lock around his spine. And as she moved the white-hot sheeting came again, with more and greater intensity, burning through her like a star going nova, consuming itself, consuming her, consuming the whole world.

Her body was locked to his, clinging to him, and he clung to her, as if nothing, *nothing* could ever part them, as the fire bathed them.

'Eve! Oh, God! Eve!' The cry broke from him, hoarse, urgent, holding in it something that pierced her. His hands released her wrist, and suddenly he was wrapping his arms around her, and she was around him, clutching at each other with an intensity that overwhelmed her even as the pulsing of her body ebbed away.

For one long, endless moment he held her as she clutched at him, holding him so close that every part of her body touched his, fused to his.

'Eve—' He breathed again, and said something to her in a language she did not know, the words halting and rasping.

Slowly, in the exhausted aftermath of passion, he lifted his weight from her. Slowly, jerkily, he extracted a hand to smooth her tumbled hair.

What was in his eyes as he looked down at her glowed through. She felt her heart turn over, even though it was still pounding in her chest like a hammerhead. What had happened? Dear God, what had happened? The question ran through her, but she could not answer—would not answer. She only knew that *something,* something so miraculous, so wonderful had happened that it would light the rest of her life for her.

She gazed up at him.

'Alexei—' she breathed.

And smiled.

And in that moment she saw his eyes change. Saw the warmth drain from him. Saw everything drain from them. Abruptly, as if a chain had been jerked, he pulled free of her, rolling over and getting to his feet in one swift, rejecting movement.

For one moment she gazed up at him, dismay etching her features.

He looked down at her, and as he did she felt ice form in her stomach. Then, without a word, he walked into the bathroom.

Alexei stared at his reflection over the basin, his hands curving over the edge of the porcelain in a death grip. In his chest he could feel his heart, still racing from the exertion—emotional and physical—it had gone through. Was still going through. His breath rasped in his lungs as he sucked air in, staring at his own stark, whitened face in the mirror.

Emotion pounded through him. Bitter and vicious.

God in heaven, how had she made such a fool of him? How had she got past his guard? He hadn't been going to touch her—had not intended to lay a finger on her corrupt, tempting body! But she'd broken through his guard as if it had been flimsy paper, setting fire to it—to him—and scorching him to the bone!

His body drenched with heat—the heat that had burned through him as he'd taken his possession of her, felt her body beneath him, felt it close around him, warm and pulsing, felt her legs lock around him, her arms clutch around him, locking him to her.

Felt himself pour into her, body and soul.

It had been everything he had ever dreamed of, fantasised about with her! Everything and more, so much more.

Until, with cold, sickening horror, he'd realised what she had done. Had seen it in her smile—her smile of victory. Triumph.

Victory over the man she'd manipulated. Triumph over the man she'd made a fool of.

Making a mockery of everything he thought it had been, everything he had hoped against hope it had been. That he had been wrong about her, that he *must* have been wrong about her! Anger—more than anger—cold, implacable fury—bit through him. Eve Hawkwood, with her beautiful, corrupt body, had made a fool of him.

A cold, hard light showed in his dark eyes. He felt his heart rate slow to a low, relentless thud. Resolution, stark and pitiless, steeled within him.

So, Eve Hawkwood thought she'd got the better of him. Thought he'd now be putty in her tempting, tainted touch. Thought he would now, his loins sated, his senses addled, meekly hand over to her the thing she wanted. The thing she had overcome all his resistance of her to obtain.

Well, that was a mistake.

Her mistake.

Hardness and darkness closed over him.

She thought she had dragged him down to her level. Now the tables would turn. He would use her corruption against her. She would learn the mistake she had made—he would teach it to her in a way she would never be able to deny. The only way that would get the message home to her. Then, and only then, could he throw her from him and be free of her.

For the briefest second repugnance showed in his eyes, then it was gone. No room for that. No room for anything except what he now had to do.

He stepped away from the basin, reaching for a towel to wrap around himself.

Eve's hands were shaking, fumbling as she tried to pull on her skirt. She didn't care about her pants or bra, let alone her stockings. She just had to get her suit skirt and jacket on, put on her shoes, grab her handbag and run—run as far and as fast as she could.

She knew she should confront him, knew she should not leave until she had got him to accept the cheque for Beaumont. But she couldn't face him again. She just couldn't.

She would write out the cheque in the hotel lobby, and leave it in an envelope for him at the front desk. Then she would run.

Run for her life. Her sanity.

Dear God, what had she just done? Emotion shook through her. How could she have responded to him like that? How could she have poured herself out for him like that? Her whole body, her whole being, transformed into a living flame of ecstasy for him?

And how—bitter gall soured her mouth, her mind—how could she have possibly, for a second, an instant, have thought as she had, so stupidly, so insanely, as she'd lain gazing up at him, her body still incandescent from that shattering, incredible experience, thought she had seen in his eyes…?

No! She had seen nothing in his eyes—*nothing.* It had been an illusion, an idiocy, a self-delusion that had made her think, *want* to think, that somehow—miraculously—the man she had thought Alexei Constantin to be when he had kissed her that very first time was the reality. Was the man whose passionate, searing embrace had taken her to a paradise she had never thought existed.

Well, Alexei Constantin was *not* that man. No miracle had occurred. It had been—as that first magical kiss had been—nothing but an illusion. Crueller than anything she had endured before.

She had seen it, seen with her own eyes as his eyes had changed. Changed from those of a man caught in the throes of sexual satiation, to the eyes of one who could not wait to get up and walk away from the female body upon which he'd slaked his own.

Pain lacerated through her. She ignored it. She had to. All she had to do was go on with what she was doing—urgently, desperately, getting herself to a state of minimum decency so she could get out of this room, out of this suite.

'Thinking of going some place?'

The voice was pleasant, almost conversational.

Eve turned, jerking upright, hands frozen in the act of zipping her skirt.

Alexei had come out of the bathroom. A towel was snaked around his hips, white against the olive of his skin.

There was a strange opaque blackness in his eyes.

It raised the hair on the nape of her neck.

'The condition of sale, Eve, was that you spend the night with me. And now that you have so…' he paused minutely '…successfully changed my mind, that's what I require. The whole night. You see—' the nape of her neck crawled '—I don't like to be short-changed. The whole night, Eve—or no sale.'

He was walking towards her. She couldn't move.

'Now,' he said, and his voice was still pleasant, still conversational, 'let's get rid of this, shall we?'

His hands came loosely around her waist to unzip the skirt. She dropped her hands away as if his were red-hot, and the skirt slithered to the ground.

Her heart had started to beat in slow, ugly slugs. Something was wrong. More wrong than it had ever been. Every instinct told her, every nerve screamed at her.

'No.' The word came from her. Not emotional, because she was beyond that now, not hysterical, not fearful. Just a negation, that was all.

'No?' He looked down at her in some mild surprise. 'But I thought you wanted me to sell your house back to you?'

'You said the deal was off.' Her voice was flat. She took a step backwards, instinctive, automatic. He stood very still.

'Well, the deal's back on, Eve. Isn't that what you wanted?' There was the same mild surprise that scraped on her nerves like fingernails in a velvet glove.

Wanted? The word mocked her. She *wanted* a deal like the one he'd offered her? She felt hysteria bite in her throat then, and yet something overrode it.

It was the expression in his eyes. They were blank—quite blank. She'd seen them blank before, but not like this. Not with this dark opacity, as if something had left him.

Or moved into him.

'So, Eve, which is to be?' The light, conversational tone chilled through her. She felt sick suddenly. Sick deep, deep in her core. 'Do you continue with my offer, or do you leave empty-handed?'

Empty-handed. The words tolled through her. She could go now, and Beaumont would be lost. Alexei Constantin would not sell to her. It would have all been for nothing.

Bleakness filled her. A bleakness that scoured her, emptying her out like a hollow shell.

I thought we had shared something amazing, but I was wrong. Wrong as I was wrong from the very beginning.

She stood very still a moment. Then, with the slightest moistening of her suddenly dry lips, she said, 'If I stay the night you'll sell Beaumont back to me?'

A smile flickered at his mouth. She felt the sickness in her stomach again.

'You have my word—and I always keep my word, Eve. Trust me on that.'

He stepped towards her again. She forced herself not to move. To stand exactly where she was. Even though suddenly, beneath the cool silk of her slip, her body felt even colder.

'Now,' he said, and he reached for her hand, taking it loosely in his and starting to lead her forward, 'what you gave me just now was very good, very invigorating—and it certainly persuaded me to renew my offer to you—but it wasn't, for all that, what I was after. It wasn't…' He paused, and she saw again the strange darkness of his eyes. A faint flicker crawled over her skin. 'What I had in mind.'

He had led her over to the foot of the bed. The cover was still on, though ruffled and indented from where, such a short time ago, she had thought the most amazing experience of her life had occurred.

'Up you go,' he said. His voice was soft. He lifted her up as if she weighed no more than a feather.

Her breath caught at the movement. And then froze in her veins as his hands smoothed around her waist.

'On your knees, Eve,' said Alexei Constantin, in the same light, pleasant voice.

Rain was sweeping over London. Eve could hear the swish of the early-morning traffic through the water on the road.

She was alone. Lying on the bed, her eyes staring upwards,

but she wasn't seeing anything. She could hear the wind-blown rain spattering on the window, but her eyes were blank.

She lay, very still, not moving.

Alexei was walking. Walking with swift, rapid strides along the deserted pavements in the cold, wet dawn as the rain descended in rods. It plastered his hair to his bowed head, trickling down his neck in chill rivulets. His suit was soaked, his face running with the rain that was stinging his face like bullets.

Perhaps, if he kept walking long enough, the rain might clear his skin.

The shower he'd taken after he'd finished with Eve Hawkwood hadn't. He'd stood under its pounding, but it had not cleaned his skin.

It had not cleaned any part of him.

He would never, he knew, feel clean again.

Cold lapped at her, but still Eve did not move. If she moved she would feel her body. Know that it still existed.

But what did it matter if it existed or not? Nothing—no power on earth or in heaven—could undo what her body had done.

What had been done to it.

Hands cupping her, smoothing over the silky fabric of her slip, her bare, sensitive skin, sliding the material of her slip upwards in silky folds to reveal the ripe, rounded mounds presented to him, then splaying over her, shaping and kneading her, sensually, sensuously, pressing softly, insistently, down on her spine while he gave her instructions to go down for him, still in that light, conversational voice, so that she sank submissive, yielding, her head twisting, cheek indenting the covers of the bed, forearms stretched, as if imploringly, her palms flattening, displaying herself to him as he stood behind her, naked and sexually aroused.

Hands kneading and shaping her, and then gliding between her thighs, smoothing and stroking, the tips of his fingers grazing

lightly, skilfully, so skilfully, over the swollen, dampening flesh
pursing beneath his touch, his skilled, deadly, arousing touch. Until
she was whimpering softly, incoherently, as she dewed for him and
he softly, sensually, eased his hands to widen the parting of her
thighs and glide his forefinger along her glistening satin folds,
ripening her, readying her, while her aching, whimpering moans
came again and again, more and more desperate, as his gliding
fingers skilfully, so skilfully, softly vibrated her exposed and
swollen bud, bringing her closer, ever closer…closer…to that point
where she must orgasm around his dewed, arousing fingertip. Until,
still vibrating her, still arousing her, he positioned himself and with
one swift, powerful movement gripped her hips and sank himself
to the hilt in her opened, throbbing flesh.

She had climaxed immediately, overpoweringly, unstoppably,
as his surging stroke engorged in her, plunging into her over and
over again as he stood behind her, prostrated for him, presenting
herself to him as he scythed into her and she surged in orgasm.

'Good, Eve—very good,' he had told her, stroking his hands
over her bared back. 'But now something for me, I think.'

He'd pulled from her, splaying her down on the bed as he did
so, then turned over her limp, still throbbing body. He'd stood,
looking down at her a moment, fully aroused still, with that same
strange darkness in his eyes.

'The night is young, Eve. What shall we do next? I think we'll
have time for everything, don't you?'

And there had been time—time for every position imaginable.
Time for orgasm after orgasm, so sustained, so intense that it had
been simply one long, endless fusion, without rest or respite. For
even in those brief periods in which Alexei Constantin had
renewed, recovered his spent potency, he had not spared her. She
had been aroused over and over and over again, with mouth, with
tongue, with skilled, gliding fingers, her body turned and tuned,
parted and positioned, until she had been one ceaseless, quiver-
ing mesh of sensation from which she could not escape.

He had spared her nothing—saying things to her, doing things to her, giving her instructions and commands and praising her. Yet not once had she felt again that moment of communion that had been there the first time. This—this was very, very different.

And her body had responded. She had not been able to resist what he was doing to her, wanting from her, no matter what he did, what he wanted. She had not been able to stop her body physically responding. That had been the horror of it.

When he had finally risen from the bed he had leant over her, smoothed the hair away from her cheek, and said to her pleasantly, appreciatively, 'That was good, Eve, very good indeed. And I will, indeed, keep my word to you. I'll sell you what you want to buy. But…' He'd paused, trailing the backs of his fingers along her cheek and looking down at her from dark blank eyes. 'For twice the sum you've offered.'

He'd straightened, still looking down at her. His face shadowed in the dim light of the room.

'Let me know tomorrow if you can meet the new price—you can reach me at my offices. Oh, and Eve—' he'd flicked a lock of her hair, lightly, carelessly '—don't think to persuade me otherwise on this by your usual means. I've had my fill of you. Or should that be…' a smile had twisted at his lips '…the other way round?'

He had strolled away, heading for the bathroom, the long, lean muscled length of his naked body limned with light. Then, at the door, he'd turned.

'What's it to be, Eve, I wonder? Will it be no sale for lack of cash? Or do you think you can raise the extra money for tomorrow? Do you think you're worth that kind of investment? Do you think, in fact—' his voice had changed, the light, conversational tone edged like the blade of a razor drawn over her throat '—you're worth anything at all?'

CHAPTER EIGHT

ALEXEI sat in the wide leather seat in the first class compartment of the flight to New York and opened his laptop. He had a dozen things to do—a hundred.

He did none of them.

Instead he stared at the blurred screen in front of him, awaiting his password. His mind was not working well this morning.

It seemed to be locked in some kind of loop. The loop that had been going round and around in his head, replaying endlessly, ever since he had walked through the rain wet streets, seeking the refuge of his deserted offices where he could spend the night in solitude.

But there was a companion with him he could not get rid of. It was there now, at his side.

Inside him.

It tore at him with jagged teeth, painful and devouring.

Self-disgust. Total, consuming self-disgust.

How had he let himself do what he had done?

I should not have touched her. I should not have gone near her. I let my anger and my shame at being so vulnerable to her deceiving, tempting beauty make me want to get the better of her. Make me want to turn the tables on her, to lead her on so that she thought she would triumph yet again over me, as she had already, overcoming my resistance to her. To make her think she was suc-

*ceeding and then to turn on her and make her see, brutally, ruth-
lessly, how her efforts had been in vain. To grind them in her face
and let her taste the bitter knowledge that I am the one man she
cannot manipulate or make a fool of, cannot corrupt.*

But she *had* corrupted him. She had taken him down to her
level, and even though he knew that he had done what he had
merely to make the bitterness of her defeat even more galling to
her, yet that didn't make it right.

The knowledge of it, the memories of it, would be with him
all his life.

And nothing, *nothing* could take that away.

His hands fisted in his lap.

*Oh, God, why did I do it? Why didn't I just throw her aside
like the garbage she is and walk out? Why did I try and win over
her? She is worth nothing—nothing at all. I should have walked
out and left her to rot.*

Slowly, he forced his hands to unfist. Slowly, he made himself
open his eyes. Well, Eve Hawkwood would rot now. He was done
with her. Finished. She was an object of disgust and contempt,
nothing more. And he would, he *must* use the knowledge, the
memory of last night, to take away the last frail remnants of the hope
he had once had. Never again would he remember Eve Hawkwood
in her beauty—only in her corruption, the way he had left her.

He stared out through the porthole into the bright, blinding
light of the sun, wanting it only to burn something from him.

But it was not just his self-disgust he wanted burnt from him.
Something much worse, much more agonising.

I could have fallen in love with her...

I could have loved her...

But now she was lost to him for ever.

Eve sat on the train, staring out of the window as the stations
of west London flashed by. Through the glass of the window

the suburbs gave way to fields and woods, glorious in their fresh summer foliage. Reservoirs glinted alongside verdant golf courses.

She saw none of it.

She had withdrawn, she knew, somewhere deep inside her mind. Somewhere that allowed her outward self to operate, to function—to go through the ticket barrier, board the train, take her seat, fold her hands neatly in her lap—but which did not allow her inward mind any space at all.

It got her home, back to Beaumont. It got her through the horrible, bitter ordeal of telling her mother that she had not been able to buy Beaumont back, the ordeal of watching her mother's face break into anguish. It got her through the ordeal of discussing with her, with the clinic's staff, what their options now were.

'AC International may let us rent the property,' she said carefully, neutrally, 'but they may just evict us. It would be best if we prepare for the latter. I will contact the estate agents to see if there is another property that would do for us.'

Deliberately, she'd ignored her mother's ashen face, the gasps of dismay from everyone. Instead, she'd simply phoned as many estate agents as she could find, and set them searching for a new home for the clinic. Alexei Constantin would evict them, she knew. He would evict them without hesitation, without compunction.

Because he was a man without conscience, without compassion.

A man like her father. Exactly like her father.

She had to forget him and get on with her life. There was nothing else left to do.

'I see. Thank you for informing me. Good day.'

Eve hung up. Then she turned to the plump middle-aged woman standing beside her—Mrs Deane, who managed the clinic.

'It's happened. It's going on the market tomorrow. The agency said to expect potential buyers at short notice.'

Her voice was clipped, unemotional. The other woman looked resigned.

'Well, you warned us it would happen. But I couldn't help hoping, that it wouldn't actually happen.' She gave a heavy sigh.

'We've had nearly three months' grace since we were given notice,' Eve said grimly. 'At least it's given us enough time to find an alternative site.'

The other woman shook her head. 'But it's going to cost so much to make it suitable, and the location is nowhere near as perfect as here. Much noisier, much less land.'

'It's the best I could find, ' said Eve tightly. She could not refute a single criticism, but there had been no alternative. They'd had to have somewhere to go when the blow fell.

And now it had fallen.

'And as for the effect on your mother…' Mrs Deane's voice had dropped, and she shook her head again.

'I know,' said Eve, in the same tight, clipped voice. 'But she's accepted it. She's had to. We've all had to. We've no choice.'

Just as she had no choice but to live with what had happened. Nothing could undo it. Nothing could take it away from her the burden of knowledge, of memory, that haunted her night after night.

When the dreams came.

She dreaded them with a sick terror. The dreams that came night after night, forcing her to relive every moment she had spent with Alexei. In the daytime she could retreat into that small, inner space where she could stop herself from remembering. Answering the phone, writing letters, talking to estate agents, attending to the million tasks that kept the clinic going.

But at night there was no such shelter.

At night he came again, time after time, and in her dreams the sweet excitement of that first joining, the blazing emotion that she had thought she'd glimpsed oh, so briefly, turned once more into the cold, dark, relentless gaze of a stranger who turned love-making into sex—sex of the most corrupt kind.

She would wake, sweating, stomach churning, heart racing, recalling once again that both dreams were crushed. Beaumont was gone and so was any hope that Alexei was the man she had thought him to be in the first moments of their meeting.

The man who had for a brief, shining moment, when they'd kissed beneath the moon and the stars, offered her a glimpse of paradise was the same one who had destroyed her dreams. The man she now loathed with every atom of her being, every cell in her body. Every waking, dreaming moment.

Alexei glanced up from the report he was reading as the car glided smoothly along the motorway. It had been hard to pay attention to the report's contents, but then these days he found it hard to pay attention to anything. A bleak greyness lay like a thin covering over him. He closed his eyes momentarily. Tiredness pricked at the backs of his eyes. He was not sleeping well.

Impatiently he opened his eyes again, and focussed them brutally on the page of type in front of him, forcing himself to concentrate. The report had been presented to him by the director of a medical research laboratory he'd just visited in Oxford, though reading it was not necessary. He'd already made the decision to fund the research. It was well worth the investment.

Yet, despite the decision, his mood was black. It should not be. He had, after all, received good news only a handful of days ago. News he'd been waiting for with grim patience.

Giles Hawkwood's destruction was complete. The message he'd received from his South American agents, who'd been keeping tabs on his target, had been conclusive.

And with the news that he had waited all his adult life to hear, surely he could now achieve closure? Be free, after so long, of the foul taint that the name Hawkwood had laid over his life? He had freed himself of the daughter, exposing her for what she was, ensuring that he never again was tempted by her. And now, finally, he was free of the father as well.

You've got to move on. Move on with the rest of your life.

Except that there was, after all, it seemed to him, very little to move on into. Oh, he could finally do what he had always intended to do with his wealth, once its purpose to destroy Giles Hawkwood had been achieved. Already he had started to put it to good use. But now, with Hawkwood destroyed, there was so much more he could do with it. Such as funding the cancer research he had decided on today. And there was no shortage of such ventures. His forward investment portfolio was crammed with enterprises that needed money, and from which the world would benefit.

It should be so simple.

And yet…

The pain of loss laced through him again, as it did so often now.

How can I feel pain at losing something I never had? She never existed, the woman I thought she was, so how can I feel pain about her? I know what the reality is—the other does not exist. Never existed.

Yet it did not matter how much he repeated that, memory came all the same. Not the final memory of Eve Hawkwood, revealed in all her true corruption, but the memory he'd first had of her. As precious as it was illusory.

Moonlight on the dark water. Soft music playing. Her hair laced with moonbeams. So fair, so very fair.

Her eyes like pools of silver. Eyes to drown in.

The quicksilver of her slender body, scarcely in his arms, like gossamer.

The sweetness of her scent.

The honey of her lips.

It was not a memory. It was an illusion. A glamour set to tempt him, beguile him, ensnare him, promising what was not there. What had never been there.

A bleak, drained look formed in his face. Eve Hawkwood embraced her own corruption willingly, wantonly, like a true voluptuary, giving herself to it, revelling in it. While Ileana—

No! Yet again his mind sliced shut. That way lay madness.

Ileana's spirit could rest now. Her suffering was over and her destroyer destroyed.

Slowly, very slowly, Alexei felt his muscles untense.

And yet the bleakness did not leave his eyes. How many like Giles Hawkwood were there in the world? How many Ileanas?

He knew the answer, and it chilled him to the soul.

Thousands. Millions.

Alexei felt the familiar crushing weight of depression press down upon him. Even with all the money he'd made there was still so little that he could do.

And yet to give in to despair was to give in to the overpowering forces ranged against him. And that he must never do. Hadn't he vowed, that day he'd left Dalaczia—boarding the ferry to Brindisi with a hundred others looking for a better life in the rich countries of Europe, as Ileana must have done before her illusions were ripped from her and she was tipped into the hell out of which death had been the only escape—hadn't he vowed that day to fight with all his strength, with all his will, those who had taken Ileana from him, however rich they were, however powerful? He had vowed to fight them with their own weapons— wealth and power—and to destroy them.

It might be beyond anyone to destroy them all—all the Giles Hawkwoods of this world, all their creatures, all their kind—and he could not save all those that such men destroyed, but those that he *could* save, he would. Ileana he had not been able to save, but there were others—so many others.

He felt the sleek, chauffeured car slow down fractionally as a car pulled across the motorway lane ahead of it, and he glanced out of the tinted windows. A junction sign flashed by, and he frowned momentarily. The name was familiar, and he wondered why. Then it came to him. It was the town nearest to the property that Eve Hawkwood had sought to buy from him with her body. The property that acted as the private rehab clinic for her lush of a mother.

He'd given instructions for it to be sold, and had thought no more about it. He frowned. Had it been sold yet? And what if it hadn't?

An English country house run as a clinic, remotely situated, yet conveniently close to London for its rich, dissolute clients to sober up discreetly. Could it be suitable for his own purposes? Those he reclaimed from hell all too often needed medical treatment, and all needed shelter and support—somewhere safe, away from the cruel, condemning eyes of the world. It might be worth considering. Perhaps he should take a look for himself.

Abruptly, he flicked the intercom to his driver. 'Maitland, take the next exit, please.'

Eve was sitting at the PC in the bookroom overlooking the gravelled drive as the sun shone on the warm brick façade of the house. It was a glorious summer's day, the grounds looking at their lushest in an English bounty of foliage and flowers, and she longed to be out in the fresh air. Especially now. Anguish bit at her. Very soon now, Beaumont would be lost to them, and she would be barred for ever from its woods and grounds.

But going out into the gardens was impossible. There were a hundred things to be done—bills to pay, letters to write, files to sort. Even with the money she had saved up over the years, without her father's monthly allowance money was punishingly tight. She herself was doing the work of three, to save money on administrative salaries and focus it on clinical staff.

Yet she welcomed the work. It kept her functioning.

Kept her going.

Her hands paused suddenly on the keyboard. Was that the sound of a car coming along the drive from the road? She stood up, crossing to the window and looking out. Only strangers came to the front. Could it be prospective buyers, as she'd been warned? A sleek, black, top-of-the-range saloon was pulling up, and a driver was emerging.

She had no premonition. None at all. But as the driver held open the passenger door and she saw who was climbing out she felt her brain congeal, the blood stop in her veins. There was a drumming sound in her head, a darkness dimming her eyes. Her hand clutched at the curtain and she could feel herself sway.

It can't be—it can't be.

The hollow, hopeless denial tolled uselessly in her mind.

Then into the drumming faintness something forced its way, surging up from the depths of her being, so overwhelming in its strength that it had taken her over before she even knew it was happening. It possessed her.

Body and soul.

She wheeled about, striding towards the bookroom door, pulling it open, and emerging into the panelled hall beyond. She strode across the chequered floor, her face frozen as if carved from stone. Without pausing in her stride she yanked open the heavy front door and stepped outside.

Alexei Constantin was poised to place his foot on the lowest of the shallow flight of stone steps that led to the front door.

'Get out of here before I call the police!'

Her voice was thick with fury, her face rigid with rage.

Alexei froze, disbelievingly.

What the hell was Eve Hawkwood doing here?

The question burned through his mind. He hadn't had the least expectation of finding her here. If he had, he'd never have come within a hundred miles of the place!

The answer came hard on the heels of his shock, sending yet another shockwave rippling through him.

Was this where *she* holed up for rehab, as well as her alcoholic mother? He might not have seen anything of a habit, but that didn't mean she didn't abuse her body with drugs as eagerly as she abused it in other ways. For a woman like Eve Hawkwood, any form of corruption would be embraceable.

His eyes narrowed.

She looked as if she were on something right now. Her face was contorted, eyes flaring. She looked half demented.

The other half—

No—he slammed shut his mind. He'd spent months trying to erase all memory of Eve Hawkwood. He'd never wanted to set eyes on her for the rest of his life. She was far, far too dangerous for him to do so.

And now she was a mere two metres away from him.

Dressed in nothing but a T-shirt and a cotton skirt. No designer label, true, but nonetheless incredibly enticing.

The kick to his guts he felt on seeing her was devastating. He felt himself reel with the blow.

Desperately he fended it off, reminding himself that the Eve Hawkwood who stood there had never, not for a single, brief, illusionary second, been the woman he'd once so fleetingly thought she was. She wasn't that magical, ethereal girl he'd held in his arms on a moonlit night, who'd caught at him as no other woman ever had.

It was the woman standing in front of him now who was real. The woman who had offered him her body to get what she wanted without the slightest hesitation, who'd thought nothing of it—who, when denied, had simply pressed her naked body against his, mocking his resistance to her, and who had gone on to mock his own determination to make her face up to her own corruption by setting him no limits, instead matching him move for move, all night long.

Had she been high that night in London? He hadn't noticed, but she certainly could be now. Or why else was she here? He placed his foot decisively on the step, noting that Maitland, who was also one of his bodyguards, was standing quietly, but ready to move, a few feet away. Why else had she slung such an absurdity at him as she had just now?

'I told you! Get the hell out of here or I'll call the police!'

The furious absurdity came again, her eyes flashing, face still contorted.

Alexei ignored her, simply nodding at Maitland. The man stepped up.

'Step away, if you please, miss,' he said dispassionately.

Eve Hawkwood's head whipped towards him, and then back to Alexei.

'You may be our landlord, Mr Constantin, but English law requires a landlord to give forty-eight hours' notice, in writing, if he wants access to his property. Come back when you've got it.'

Alexei's face was expressionless. At his side, Maitland inclined his head slightly and murmured to him in a low voice. Alexei nodded.

Before Eve realised what was happening, her arms had been taken in a hold that was as immobilising as it was shocking.

Alexei Constantin walked past her and through the wide open door of the house.

'Are you prepared not to be obstructive, miss?' enquired Maitland.

Her body was rigid, completely rigid. 'If you do not release me immediately I will cite assault! Do you understand me?'

Eve's voice was icy, but she'd slammed the lid down on her fury.

She was released, but as she strode back inside the man stuck to her side like a shadow. He was presumably some kind of minder. She was familiar with the type. Dispassionate, unemotional, and quietly brutal to the extent the law permitted.

But what the law did *not* permit—for she had checked it specifically now that her mother no longer owned Beaumont—was landlords having automatic right of access to a property that was tenanted.

Alexei Constantin was standing in the middle of the hall, looking about him.

'I've told you once,' Eve announced. 'If you don't leave I will phone for the police. You have *no* right of access.'

Alexei ignored her tirade. In a clipped voice he merely said, 'Maitland, find whoever's in charge and tell them that Miss Hawkwood requires medical assistance.'

The bodyguard nodded, cast an assessing look at Eve, and headed for the corridor leading off from the hall.

Alexei turned fully to Eve. His look was measured. Expressionless. But something in his eyes, that strange darkness she had seen only once before, made the pincers claw in her stomach.

He spoke, each word hitting her like blows.

'I suggest you return to whatever part of the building you came from and resume whatever therapy you've been put on. Your mother may once have owned this house, but *you,*' Alexei informed her coldly, 'have never been anything more than a patient here.'

'Patient…' The word was breathed from her uncomprehendingly. She stared blankly.

He ignored her, just going on in the same cold, killing tone, 'Presumably they allow you to run wild here on the strength of your mother's previous ownership of the clinic. But letting you roam round when you're high is—'

Eve's face contorted. Something exploded inside her, shattering every last vestige of the control that she had hammered down over her life.

'*Get out!* Take your disgusting, filthy carcass and get out of here!' The words ripped from her. More came, tearing out of a part of her that had been suffocated for far too long and which was now possessing her utterly. It burst out of her, unstoppable, like hot, burning lava. 'Call back your bully-boy minder and get off these premises. Now. Right now. You've got no right to be here. None. And even if you did have a legal right, how *dare* you show up here? How dare you? My God, I should hand you over to the tabloids for what you've done. They'd tear you to shreds. Evicting us like this after we tried to buy back the house at a fair price. But I won't do it—I won't upset my mother. She's suffered enough, God only knows. And I won't give you the chance to throw your vile, disgusting mud at me. What you made me do—'

She choked, convulsing. 'My God, what you made me do…'

With two strides Alexei Constantin had closed the distance and clamped his hands around her upper arms. His face was savage.

'What *I* made you do?' He snarled the words at her. 'I didn't *make* you do anything. You did it willingly, eagerly—you were all over me. So don't try and hide behind that lily-white façade of yours. You're as corrupt as your scum of a father. And I've got the proof of that. There wasn't *anything* you wouldn't do.'

She went rigid.

'Are you *insane?*' Her voice was a rasp, horror and disbelief mingled.

The hands clamped harder around her arms. His voice hissed down at her, vicious in its denunciation. His eyes scored into her.

'Is that what you'd like?' he demanded, mouth contorting. 'To exonerate yourself by going for denial? Well, let me remind you of just what you went along with—anything and everything, so long as it got you what you wanted. And don't deny you enjoyed it. You came again and again and again. With everything we did. *Everything!* So don't think you can stand there and look virtuous and outraged, because I know *exactly* what you really are—a woman who will do anything with a man—or men, or women, or both together. Who knows what you wouldn't stoop to just to get what you want.'

She could feel the blood leaching from her face. Faintness drummed in her ears.

Where she found the strength from she didn't know. She pulled his hands from her and jerked away.

She wanted to run—run as fast and as far as she could. But she couldn't run. She had to face this—face it and face Alexei Constantin, who had drowned her in a bottomless well, a sickening cesspit, and was now, with a callousness so despicable that she could not believe it, telling her that she had wanted, *wanted* that night to happen.

'I did what I had to do,' she said, and her voice was very strange. 'You made it very, very clear that you would not sell Beaumont unless I had sex with you. So that's what I had to do.'

'You *had* to do it?' His scathing, jeering voice echoed hers, cutting like a knife across her skin. 'For what?' He gestured around him with a cutting slash of his hand. 'For a pile of bricks and mortar? Your mother's own personal drying-out clinic? And your personal drug rehab clinic as well, it seems. That's your other little secret, isn't it, Eve? You like to do the little white lines just as you like to do the between-the-sheets action! Tell me—does it make the sex better? Is that it? Do you get a double orgasm—one from the drugs, one from the sex? But you don't like anyone to know, do you, Eve? You like to keep that lily-white image of yours pristine and perfect, don't you? But I know better. And how many other men, Eve? Not just the ones your father picked out for you, but the ones you pick for yourself as well. How many know just what you'll do to get what you want? Is that what's made you angry now? Because on me it didn't work? You didn't get what you wanted from me? You didn't get to keep your personal, private, family clean-up clinic? Is that it, Eve?'

Her body was like glass, so brittle that the slightest movement must surely shatter it into a million shards.

And yet it did not shatter.

'Our personal, private, clean-up clinic? That's what I wanted to buy back from you?' She could feel the tension knotting every muscle in her body. It made her voice high-pitched, strange— but very calm. Incredibly, unnaturally calm.

'You don't like me calling it that, do you, Eve?'

His voice was scathing, but it did not cut her.

'No,' she said. It was all she said.

Then she indicated a pair of double doors to his right. She walked towards them. Still she did not shatter. She opened them and walked through. They led into a small but elegant sitting room.

She looked back at him. Her eyes were strange.

'Come,' she said. 'Come and see.'

She crossed the room and opened a pair of French windows onto a terrace along the east face of the house. She waited expectantly, looking back towards Alexei Constantin. There was no expression on her face.

Slowly he walked across the sitting room, and stepped outdoors.

'This way,' she said, in the same strange, brittle voice.

She started to walk briskly towards the corner of the house. Alexei followed with long, wary strides. Emotion was storming through him. What the hell was going on? What the hell was she trying now? There was nothing she could do or say that would fool him. He knew her; he *knew* what she was.

He had the evidence.

He had the memories.

He watched her reach the corner of the house and disappear around it. As he neared the corner he frowned. Something was distracting him from the tornado of emotions twisting in his mind, his guts. There seemed to be noise coming from somewhere just beyond him. A noise that seemed completely and totally out of place.

He turned the corner.

And stopped dead.

There was a lawn, covering the breadth of the house and stretching out widely to herbaceous borders and flowerbeds backed by a sheltering swathe of trees, predominantly beech, but with oaks and chestnuts and some exotic species. It was a beautifully landscaped vista.

But that wasn't what had stopping him in his tracks. Around the edge of the lawn, crossing over it and winding around the flowerbeds, were metalled pathways.

And along the pathways wheelchairs were bowling along.

Wheelchairs with children.

Some had support for their heads and arms, some had adults to push their chairs, others were propelling their own.

And the noise they made. Calling out and shouting excitedly. Laughing and chattering.

There seemed to be some sort of game going on, Alexei realised. A chasing game. Possibly with teams. He wasn't sure.

But that he knew, was because the world suddenly made no sense. Nothing made sense.

He watched as one of the wheelchairs changed direction and headed along a short pathway to the figure in a T-shirt and cotton skirt standing at the edge of the stone-paved terrace where it touched the lawn.

'Evie—Evie! Did you see? I caught Tom, and he's the fastest hotshot on wheels. I've never caught him before, and now I have. Did you see? Did you see?'

The face of the boy who'd called out was alight with pleasure and satisfaction, even though his speech was halting. The fingers of one hand spasmed, the other rested on the electric controls of the wheelchair. A neck support let him rest his head to one side.

Alexei watched Eve Hawkwood walk up to him. The boy must

be about seven or so. It was difficult to tell. There was something familiar about the boy's face.

'I saw, Charlie,' she answered him.

The high, brittle voice was gone. Almost gone. As if the effort required not to use it was so great it was impossible to achieve completely.

'It was a real chase, but you got him. I knew you'd do it. You're getting really fast now. Ace steering, too.' She ruffled his hair affectionately, then spoke again. 'Uh-oh, better get going again. I think Tom's circling round to get his revenge.'

The boy tapped the controls and smartly reversed his chair back out onto the main path, accelerating away from another boy heading towards him from the far end. Alexei watched Eve look on for a moment longer, then she turned and came back towards him. She was speaking as she walked. Her voice was back to the way it had been.

Strange. Detached. Totally, completely detached.

But calm. Very calm.

'That was Charlie,' she said. 'He's my brother. And it was for him, and the other children here, that I needed to buy back Beaumont. To keep them safe here—' her eyes levelled to his, and there was nothing in them, nothing at all '—whatever it took to do so.'

CHAPTER NINE

SHE was still talking. Alexei heard the words, but they came from very far away. *He* was very far away. Twenty-three long, agonising years away.

'*Don't go, Illi—I shall miss you.*'

The arms around him had held him tightly.

'*I'm doing it for you, Axi. For you. And I'll come back, you'll see. I'll be wearing a beautiful dress, and I'll bring you presents. And I'll send money back, for you, so you won't have to go to the orphanage, and you can stay at school and take all your exams, and become someone that our parents would have been so proud of. Everything will be wonderful for you.*'

He'd clung to her, his ten-year-old's hands clutching her.

'*But I don't want you to go. I want you to stay.*'

She'd shaken her head. '*I can work in Italy, in France—all over the world. That's what these businessmen have told me. I can earn good money and send it home to you. So you can get the education Mama and Papa wanted for you. You know how hard it is for us here, how there is no work for me. But in Italy, in the rich countries, there is work. And it isn't even work, Axi, not like working in the fields. I shall be a singer, and wear beautiful clothes, and a rich, handsome man will fall in love with me. I'll write to you all about it, just you wait.*

*And when I've made enough money I'll come back, Axi. I'll
come back.'*

*She'd ruffled his hair, easing his arms from her, and stood up,
smiling down at him.*

*'I'll come back, Axi, to the best little brother in the world.
I promise.'*

And now, as he stood there, a grown man, another sister was
talking. A sister who, like his, had done whatever it took to keep
her little brother safe.

Had she known, Ileana, just what kind of work the businessmen visiting their village had had in mind for her? He didn't
know. He had never known.

Because he had never seen her again.

But Eve Hawkwood had known what he had wanted of her.
He'd spelt it out very clearly. And she had done it. Done it over
and above all his expectations.

She was still speaking in the same calm, strange voice. The
words went through him, each one a deadly, mortal bullet.

"We have around twenty-five children here at any one time.
Including Charlie. He has cerebral palsy because he was born
prematurely, after my mother went into labour after my father
had subjected her to one of his periodic beatings. My father
agreed to fund what you see here in return for evading prosecu-
tion for assault. I made sure of it. Having other children here
helps both of them, because we can provide specialist treatment
plus either permanent or respite care, and it helps Charlie because
it gives him friends as well as family and clinical treatment. It's
a good place for them—lots of grounds and space, and an all-
weather swimming pool, which they adore. They'll be sad to
move, because the new house I've bought with the money I was
going to use to buy Beaumont back hasn't got a pool, or nearly
as much space. It isn't adapted as yet for wheelchair access, and
I'll need to spend money kitting out treatment rooms. There'll

be less staff too, as I've had to let some go since I lost the allowance my father paid—'

She broke off, falling silent suddenly. Her eyes went past him, and her expression changed, became alarmed.

Alexei turned his head. Maitland was approaching from the far end of the terrace, walking beside a slim, middle-aged woman wearing an impeccably cut dark grey skirt and a black twin-set. As they drew closer, Alexei recognised her. The Honourable Amabel Hawkwood lacked her daughter's silvered beauty, but she had the kind of fair, well-bred good-looks that women of her class so often had. Her fine-boned face was strained, however, and Alexei could see the tension in her.

'Mr Constantin?' The modulated tones sounded uncannily like her daughter's. 'How do you do? I'm Amabel Hawkwood. I'm so sorry. I didn't realise you would be arriving today.'

She held out a hand to him, and automatically he found himself shaking it.

'It was an impromptu decision,' he said. 'I apologise for any inconvenience.'

He sounded abrupt, he knew. But it was hard to make his voice work. It was hard to make anything work. It was as if an earthquake had just happened, and no one else had noticed.

'Not at all,' replied Amabel Hawkwood in her crystal-cut tones. 'Would you like some coffee? Or would you just like to look around? Or…?'

She seemed at a loss as to what to say next.

Alexei found himself looking at her with the part of his brain that still seemed to be functioning. There was a haunted look in the faded eyes, the face was too thin, the pose of her head too tense. She was exerting considerable self-control, he could sense it. A self-control that was demanding more of her than she could sustain.

And yet she would sustain it. She would not collapse. She would not allow the tension and stress racing through her to become visible. She would continue to appear very composed, very restrained. Totally self-controlled.

No matter what was happening to her.

He could feel ice start to form in his spine. Chilling him with icy fingers, splaying out into every nerve-end.

Amabel Hawkwood's daughter had stood in front of him like that. Stood in front of him that evening after dinner, when he'd informed her of the conditions he was imposing before he would sell her what she wanted to buy. She had not moved; she had not changed her expression. Nothing, absolutely nothing had shown in her face.

She had simply accepted his terms.

Accepted everything he had done to her.

Everything.

He pulled his mind back viciously, violently.

His eyes flickered out over the lawn, where the wheelchairs were still racing around the paths, where the children in them were still playing their chasing game, as if their bodies worked as well as any other child's in the world.

He spoke, pulling his gaze back towards Amabel Hawkwood. Whose son, Eve's young brother, was in one of those wheelchairs.

'I'm afraid there's been a…misunderstanding.'

He could see fear flicker suddenly in her eyes, instantly suppressed. He did not let her speak, but continued, taking a sharp breath. The air seemed to cut his lungs.

'Beaumont is yours. The title deeds will be returned immediately. I will fund the salaries of any staff you had to let go, and I will purchase this other property from you and cover all associated costs. Please accept…' Did his voice falter? He hoped it did not. He hoped he was succeeding in exerting the same iron control that these two women did over their emotions. 'Please accept my profound apologies for this unfortunate misunderstanding.'

He paused just long enough to take in another cutting breath of air, and then continued.

'Will you also allow me to say one more thing which I have reason to believe you will find reassuring? You are safe, absolutely safe from your husband. Giles Hawkwood is dead.'

He watched the face in front of him lose what little colour it had, heard the muffled gasp from the woman out of his eyeline. He had tried to soften his voice, but it was hard. Everything was hard. Agonisingly hard. He turned away. He had to go. Right now. He started to walk back in the direction he'd come from, with Maitland falling into step behind him.

There were footsteps behind him—hurrying. His sleeve was seized, and he halted in his tracks.

'Are you *sure?* Are you *sure* he's dead?'

There was a vehemence in Eve's voice that made him turn and look down at her. It hurt to do so, but he did it.

'He was killed by members of the drugs cartel whose money he laundered through his company. He fled to them, but when the SFO started their investigations he was considered a risk. I've had my agents keep watch on him and they have reported his murder to me. You'll be hearing that officially soon, from the police.'

Something worked in her eyes, the first emotion he'd seen since she'd invited him to 'come and see'.

It detonated an answering emotion in him. Words burst from him.

'Eve! I didn't know about the children! I swear I didn't know!'

Urgency raked through his voice and he caught at her hand.

She yanked it away as if it were red-hot. For one long, endless moment he held her eyes, and in that one moment he tried with all his strength to pour into them everything that he knew he must convey to her.

'Eve…' His voice was low and hoarse. 'I have to speak to you. I have to…'

She turned away, walking back towards her mother, her gait

jerky, suppressing its unevenness with the sheer power of her self-control. A self-control so overpowering that it had enabled her to do what she had done.

Guilt lacerated him, tore him with claws that shredded the flesh from his bones.

I didn't know. I didn't know.

The futile litany tolled in his brain.

Bleakly, he turned away, and returned to his car.

'Is it really true? We don't have to leave here?'

Charlie's excitement was audible even through the distortion of his speaking voice. Eve watched as her mother hugged her son.

'No, we don't, darling. Isn't it wonderful? We can stay here for ever and ever now.'

Eve felt the tears prick in her eyes as she watched her mother embrace Charlie, who struggled so bravely, as did all the children here, against the harsh affliction that sought to make them prisoners within their own frail bodies.

It was not the first time that such tears had come to her. She had so much to rejoice over. The deeds to Beaumont had been received the day after Alexei's visit, together with a cheque so large it meant that they could expand what they did there. Eve's thoughts had raced ahead. A hyperbaric chamber, perhaps, where the children could breathe the highly oxygenated air which could give relief to their condition? Or more therapy rooms, where the essential physio on their stricken limbs could take place. And more clinical staff, physical and occupational therapists, speech therapists, to help the children overcome the frustration of their difficulties in the simplest tasks of moving, learning and communicating.

It was, as her mother said, wonderful.

And for her, too, Eve knew.

Her mother was a changed woman, Eve could see. Not just because the haven she had built for the child she adored was now

safe, but because *she* was safe too. The monster who had terrorised her since her wedding day was dead.

A sombre light lit Eve's eyes. She could not mourn her father.
He did not deserve it. He had brutalised and terrorised her
mother, crippled his own son and prevented his daughter from
having anything like a normal life. Love and marriage had always
been out—what man would have tolerated Giles Hawkwood for
a father-in-law?—and Eve had known she could never leave her
mother unprotected by seeking her own salvation elsewhere.

Yet love and marriage were still beyond her, even with her
father dead. She knew that. It would be a long time before she
could put behind her that night with Alexei—a night in which
she'd thought she had touched the stars before it had destroyed
her. Cold, silent bitterness filled her. What man would want her?
What man *could* want her? Not once they knew. Knew what she
had done. Knew what her memories were…

I did what was right—I had no choice but to do it. No choice.

Over and over again she would repeat the words, dropping like
stones through her brain. They made no difference. None.

*The wrong thing for the right reason. And, no matter how right
the reason, the memory of that night will never leave me.*

The simple, punishing logic ground her down, crushing her
like a weight. A weight she could never shed, would never be rid
of. It had happened. She had done it.

Her memory told her so, day after day. Her dreams told her
so, night after night.

Alexei disconnected his phone and exhaled his breath in sharp frustration. For three weeks his PA had been trying to get an appointment for him to see Eve. He had to speak to her. He just had to. It
was imperative, essential. But she was shutting him out. Totally.

His jaw tightened as he stared out of his office window across
the Mayfair street to the Georgian houses on the other side. He was

unable to travel as he needed to be in England—needed to be available the moment Eve Hawkwood gave him the opening he needed.

But she never did.

He exhaled again heavily. He was going to have to go to her, he knew. He didn't want to. Didn't want to go to the place where the truth about Eve Hawkwood had risen up like a serpent and swallowed him whole.

But if it was the only way to see her, then he would do so.

He jabbed the phone again.

'Tell Maitland I want the car in fifteen minutes.'

Eve was in the pool, helping with a swimming lesson. The children loved their swimming sessions, and the support of the water made it easier for their limbs to move. Across the pool she could see Charlie and his friend Tom, splashing away at each other and laughing excitedly.

'Eve, your mother's asking for you.'

One of the staff was beckoning to her from the pool-edge. Carefully Eve handed Leah over to one of the therapists, giving the little girl a smiling word of praise and encouragement. Then she vaulted out of the pool and headed off to get changed.

What was up? she wondered. Her mother knew she was in the pool, and wouldn't have called for her unnecessarily. A sliver of apprehension went through her. It was almost automatic. She'd lived with tension all her life, and the months since her father's flight from the UK and the threat to Beaumont had been so appalling that even now, when Beaumont seemed safe again, she still could not relax properly.

And then there was the business of Alexei Constantin trying to make contact with her.

Her face hardened. All the staff had instructions to refuse his calls.

Deliberately, she started to think about other things, going through all that needed to be done to keep Beaumont running smoothly. Her mind ran on as she entered the main part of the house and headed for her mother's sitting room. For a fraction of a second memory flashed through her. Herself marching across it, with a rage so intense it had been like a white, burning flame within her, consuming everything inside her, to throw open the French windows and plunge along the terrace.

To show him just what kind of clinic Beaumont was!

No! Don't think. Don't remember. Don't think of anything. *Anything* at all.

Anything *at all* to do with Alexei Constantin.

He did not exist. She would not allow him to exist. She *would* not.

The iron door sliced shut in her mind.

Briskly, she walked across the entrance hall and opened the door to her mother's sitting room.

Her mother was inside.

Alexei Constantin was inside.

She almost backed out. But her mother's face lit, and she smiled and said, 'Ah, Eve—there you are. Come and sit down.'

A vice seemed to have clamped over Eve's abdomen, crushing her. As if in slow motion she watched as Alexei unfolded his tall frame from the delicate antique sofa he'd been sitting on, opposite her mother, and got to his feet. She didn't look at him. Jerkily she crossed the room and hovered beside her mother on the matching sofa by the French windows.

'Mr Constantin was saying how he would very much like to see what we do here. I'm sure you'd like to show him around. It's very good of him to spare the time.'

'Not at all, Mrs Hawkwood. I've been hoping to return here under happier circumstances,' Alexei replied smoothly.

Eve's mother inclined her head briefly. She was wearing a black skirt and cashmere twinset, with her customary pearls.

Eve had said nothing when her mother had chosen to wear mourning for the husband whose pastime had been criminally assaulting her. Even in widowhood she was obeying the rules by which she had lived as a wife. Never to make a fuss, never to complain, always to do the correct thing.

Now, she heard her mother speak in a low voice. 'I am so very, very grateful to you, Mr Constantin. Legally, I know, Beaumont should belong to your company. But—'

'No.' Alexei raised a hand, and his voice had an edge to it. 'What happened with this property should *not* have happened. All I have done is rectify a situation that should not have arisen in the first place. And now, if your daughter can indeed spare the time from her duties, I would indeed be most grateful if she would—'

'I'm afraid now isn't the most convenient time.'

Eve's voice cut across his abruptly. Her mother looked at her with a shocked and disapproving expression.

'My dear, Mr Constantin is a very busy man, as well as an exceptionally generous one.' There was reproof in her voice.

Eve felt her nails dig into her palm. She would not make a scene in front of her mother. But she had to get Alexei Constantin away from here.

'Very well,' she murmured. 'If you'd like to come this way, Mr Constantin?'

Jerkily, she walked to the door and opened it. He followed her, taking his leave of her mother, then following Eve out into the entrance hall and shutting the door to the sitting room behind him.

'Eve—'

'This way, Mr Constantin.' Eve started to walk towards the main corridor that led to the rear of the house where the treatment rooms were situated.

Her elbow was caught. She froze.

'Eve, I came here to talk to you, not for a tour of the house. I *have* to talk to you.'

She turned to him. Turned on him.

Her face was quite blank.

'No, Mr Constantin, you do not need to talk to me. And if that is why you are here, I must ask you to leave.' She took a breath. 'Please let go of me.'

Her voice was rigid.

His hand dropped from her elbow. She wouldn't look at him. Instead she looked at a point just past him, her eyes unblinking.

'Eve.' His voice had that edge to it again. 'We *have* to speak. I would prefer to do so in private, but we can, if you prefer, have this conversation here. I tell you now, I won't leave without talking to you.'

She looked at him then. His face looked as if it had been cut with a knife-blade, every feature sharply outlined. For one long, silent moment she just looked at him. Not into his eyes—not that—but at his face. She couldn't think, or breathe, or do anything. Then, with a jerk, she turned away and headed for the front door.

He followed her.

She set off along the gravelled drive, but almost immediately turned off to her left, along a wide stone-paved pathway that led slightly upwards into the curve of the hill that sheltered Beaumont. Whether Alexei Constantin was following her or not she didn't care. The drip of rain from the leaves on the surrounding bushes and the cool damp air on her cheeks was all she registered.

She knew where she was going. To the little folly that was nestled into the lee of the trees, giving a vista down onto the lawns. The path steepened, and she increased her stride. A few minutes later she reached the miniature Greek temple, with its open front and a stone seat running around its square interior. It was a familiar retreat for her, ever since childhood.

Long before her brother had been born, her mother had lived at Beaumont as much as she could—when she hadn't been doing her duty as Mrs Giles Hawkwood at her husband's side. The folly had been a favourite spot in high summer, in the cool shade, with the grounds and gardens spread below.

It was also, Eve knew, completely out of earshot of the house or anyone on the lawns. She walked inside and sat herself down on the stone seat at the back, her arms folded across her.

In the entrance, the dark figure of Alexei Constantin was outlined against the grey, looming sky.

'Well?' she demanded.

Her voice, she thought, sounded commendably indifferent. Around her abdomen, however, the vice was crushing even more tightly than it had in her mother's sitting room.

For a moment he said nothing.

He glanced down at the lawns, deserted now in this weather. Then he looked back at Eve.

'Why didn't you tell me why you wanted to buy back this place?'

Was the accent more pronounced? Eve didn't know.

'I did.' Her voice was brusque.

He shook his head. 'All you said was that the property used to be your mother's, that was all. You never said what this place was used for.'

Eve's eyes widened. 'You knew it was a clinic—that fact was mentioned several times.'

His expression changed. 'A clinic—that was all that you ever said. And, like the rest of the world, I thought—' He took a sharp intake of breath. 'I thought, as gossip had it, that it was, as I said, some kind of discreet clinic where alcoholics and drug addicts could be treated in expensive privacy.'

'You mean alcoholics and drugs addicts like my mother and myself?' Eve queried harshly.

'There were rumours about your mother—that she drank too much. Now, of course, I understand why.'

He fell silent. His expression changed.

'My God, if I had *known*—if I had just *known!*' The vehemence in his voice was frightening. He strode further into the folly's interior. It seemed stiflingly small suddenly.

For a moment there was complete silence. Inside her chest Eve could hear her heart thumping with a hard, heavy thud. She looked at him. She still couldn't look into his eyes. But she looked at his face. The shadows played on it so that it was like a gaunt, grey mask.

The silence stretched, like wire to breaking point.

Suddenly he spoke.

'Forgive me. Please. Forgive me for what I did to you.' His voice was low, scarcely audible.

Eve looked at him.

'I can't,' she said.

She got to her feet. Her arms were still wrapped around herself. She felt very cold, all the way down to her bones.

'I can't forgive you,' she said. 'I can't forgive myself.'

His eyebrows snapped together.

'Your*self?*'

'Yes.' Her voice was very calm. It was as if someone else were speaking. 'I can know with my mind that what I did was morally justified. That I had no more right to the luxury of telling you to go to hell than I have the right to turn my back on my mother, on my brother, on any of the children here. That for their sake I had no choice but to do what you demanded of me. But it doesn't make any difference.' Her voice was low, almost inaudible. 'I know that I was morally justified in what I did, but I still did it. I watched my father for years, I know what men like him did for sex, how vile sex could be. And you made it just as vile that night. You made me feel the worst kind of whore. Even if I were to get amnesia, be unable to remember it, it would not mean that it did not happen. I did what I did that night. Nothing—ever—can take that away. Nothing.'

She fell silent. Slowly her eyes dropped to the stone floor. She couldn't say anything else. What else was there to say?

There was a leaf lying on the stone floor, crumpled and wind-blown. It absorbed all of her attention. She stared at it. If she just went on staring at it, it would be all right. It would be all right.

But she couldn't go on staring at it. She lifted her eyes. She could feel them lifting. Feel, as she did so, an emotion boil up in her that was like a roaring tornado in her ears. It was coming to her from a long way away, but it was getting closer. Rushing down on her, rushing over her, consuming her and possessing her. And then it was upon her, like a storm, a tempest, overpowering her, overwhelming her. A storm that had been gathering not just since she had known Alexei, but all her life.

Her face contorted. The tornado roared through her throat, her voice.

'You had no *right* to do it!' Fury, rage, righteous anger spat from her. 'No *right!* Whether I wanted this place back because of children like Charlie, or whether I wanted it back because my mother was an alcoholic—or because I was a drug addict—you had no *right* to do what you did! Nothing, *nothing* gave you that right!'

Her voice hissed like the boiling of the sea, in a hurricane of emotion, of fury.

'You made me take something that God gave us for the most perfect celebration of our physical beings and you destroyed it. And *don't* tell me that sex is natural and wholesome and a per-fectly normal appetite. Because the sex *you* wanted that night was nothing like that. It could have been something out of a porn film. And don't you *dare* tell me that porn is fine these days—totally cool, nothing to make a fuss about. That it's everywhere, and everyone does it and watches it and reads it. Because *I* don't want my sex like that. No sane, decent human being does. And you know it! Neither man nor woman! But you did! You *wanted* it to be like that! You *wanted* me to be submissive. And you know what the ultimate betrayal was? You made me take physical pleasure in it. I didn't want to. I didn't want it to be like that. And least of all did I want to take physical pleasure from it!'

A terrible, shuddering breath raked through her.

'But I couldn't stop it. I couldn't stop my body. Because that's what it's designed to do—take pleasure in sex. Because sex is supposed to be something that *celebrates* our physical nature, not something that degrades and defiles it! And don't, *don't* try and tell me I'm hung up, and neurotic, and repressed. That's not it. I just wanted it to be real, to be…' She fell silent, her voice failing.

He didn't move. Not a muscle. But there was something in his eyes, something that she could not make out in the shadowed interior. Something, for the briefest moment, that was almost like a mirror to her own eyes. Then it was gone. In its place a bleak, bare resolve.

He seemed to be steeling himself to speak, with a gritted inhalation of breath.

'Eve…' his words were halting '…I can't…undo…what I did to you. My disgust at what I did is more than you can ever know, but understand something—I…I beg you. When I…took you…like that, that night, I thought…I thought you *were* like that. I thought that *that* was the kind of woman you were already.'

She was staring at him. Staring at him in disbelief.

'You thought I was like that already?' Her voice was hollow. For a moment she could say nothing more, then emotion blazed from her. 'You *dare* to put the blame on me? To say that you thought I was that kind of woman? What the *hell* had I *ever* done to make you think I was someone like that? Why should you *possibly* think that? What *possible* evidence did you have to make you believe that? Until the day I came to your London office with the market price for Beaumont in my handbag the only thing that had happened between us was one kiss—*one kiss!* A kiss so innocent a virgin could have kissed like that! So how the *hell* did I suddenly go from that to…to the kind of woman who…who…?' Her voice twisted in revulsion.

Nausea clenched in her stomach, and she had to fight it back. He had started to speak again. His voice as expressionless as his face.

'I thought that was the kind of woman you already were because…' He paused minutely, then went on. 'Because your father offered you to me the night I dined on board his yacht.'

She could feel the blood freezing in her veins as she stared at him.

'He did what?' The words were a chill, disbelieving whisper.

A muscle worked in his cheek.

'He showed me down to your cabin. You were in bed, half naked. You might have been asleep; you might have simply been waiting for me to arrive, having been primed beforehand by your father. He thought—' his voice twisted, becoming raw and ugly suddenly '—that offering you to me might stave off the takeover.'

His voice changed again, a note of urgency in it. 'Eve—understand there have always been…rumours…about you. That you were willing to devote yourself so absolutely to your father's interests that you were prepared to…to sleep with men he considered useful to him. Men like Pierre Roflet, whose father is president of a bank which could have, if it had wanted, proved a white knight to your father in the takeover battle. Pierre was there, in the South of France…'

'You thought that of me?'

There was something in her voice that was like a knife twisting in living flesh.

'I didn't know. I didn't know you. So…' A darkness was in his voice, but she was not mindful of it. All she knew was the monstrousness of what he was saying to her. 'I decided to find out for myself. I made you that offer to see if you would refuse it. And when you did not…'

His eyes slid past her, boring into the stone wall behind her. Deadness filled his voice.

'I never intended to have sex with you. Acquit me of that, at least. I wanted only to…to test you. That's why I refused you, tried to send you home. But you didn't accept my refusal, did you? You were determined to get me to sell to you after all—to meet my "condition of sale". And so you…came on to me. And I succumbed to you.' The blood drained from his face, leaving his features gaunt and stark. 'I succumbed, gave in, could not resist you. You got the better of me—dragged me down to your level, as I thought—and I couldn't let you think you'd won. I could not let you think your wiles had twisted me, mocked my determination not to lay a finger on you after all. For a moment made me believe it was more than just the deal.' All emotion drained from his voice. 'And I did what I did to you. Deliberately made it just cold-blooded sex.'

He paused. He seemed to have difficulty speaking. Then, with a harsh breath in his lungs, he finished, 'And then I refused you what you wanted. Showed you it had all been in vain. Left you with nothing. I know it was a low blow, but I was so disgusted with myself for doing what I had done, and with you for making me like that. It was a way of striking back at you.'

There was silence. From very far away he thought he could hear the sound of children, or birdsong, or wind in the trees, or a car passing very far away along the road, beyond the woods. But otherwise silence. The silence of the dead. The damned.

Then, very slowly, he spoke, each word dragged from him as if it were carrying an unbearable weight.

'And all along you were not the woman I had thought you to be. You were a woman prepared to do whatever was…necessary…to—' He broke off, as if cut at the very roots of his being.

His face contorted again. Then suddenly new emotion blazed from him. His eyes lit. 'Oh, God, Eve, I was so completely wrong about you!'

There was a strangled sound in her voice. Her face blazed with sudden fury. She took a jerking step backwards.

'*You* were completely wrong about *me?* My God, you dare to stand there and say that to my face? Who the *hell* do you think you are to demand proof about whether those vile, disgusting *rumours* about me were true or not? About my father pimping me off? That I was some kind of promiscuous slut who would have sex with any man my father told me to—or any man I wanted something from? How *dare* you think you had *any* kind of right to subject me to some hideous *test* just to satisfy your bloody *curiosity* about me?'

She took a raking breath, rage burning through her.

'And who the *hell* do you think you are to have *any* kind of right to judge *any* woman? Do you think I starred in our little porn film all on my own? *You were there too.* And nothing forced *you* to be there. You *chose* to be there. So what the hell kind of a man does that make *you?* The kind who thinks that only *women* can be promiscuous sluts, never a man? The kind who thinks that the women who do porn are garbage, but the man who watches it, who does it with them, is squeaky bloody clean?'

She was choking with fury as the words were hurled from her like stones, like knives and daggers, or anything else she could hurl at this man who stood there and thought himself untouched by what he'd done.

'You *sicken* me. You stand there and tell me you were wrong about me? Well, I wasn't wrong about you. Pierre Roflet opened my eyes about *you* that very first evening! That woman you picked up at the bar and then walked off with wasn't a hotel guest. She was a prostitute. Pierre told me. He told me she'd just offered her services to him for cash. But that didn't bother you, did it? *Did it?* You don't have a problem paying cash for sex, just like you didn't have a problem doing what you did to me when you thought I was a whore. You're perfectly happy with either. And I thank God that Pierre told me that the girl was a prostitute. Because it shook the stupid moonlight right out of my hair and told me *exactly* what kind of man you were. The kind of man you *are!*'

Breath razored in her throat. It was hurting, hurting so much, even to breathe.

'I've had to live with that sort of life—seeing what my father did to those women. A man who uses prostitutes is beneath contempt.' Her voice was hard and merciless. 'A man who thinks he has a right to impose some kind of disgusting sexual test on me is beneath contempt. *You* are beneath contempt. And I don't ever want you coming anywhere near me again.'

She looked at him one last time.

'Get out,' she said, and there was a venom in her voice that was mortal. 'Get out of my sight. Out of my life.'

His face was a mask. The skin stretched so tight it must tear, rip, leaving nothing but the bones beneath. For a moment he struggled, as if to speak, but stayed silent. For one long, endless moment, he just looked at her. Then, bowing his head, he turned and left.

Behind him, Eve stood, her body shaking with a fine tremor.

From the shadows around her, a darkness was settling over her being.

CHAPTER TEN

Days passed. She could see them passing, filled with warmth and late summer sun. But not for her. The world seemed to be receding. The small, dim place in her mind where she lived seemed to be shrinking. She did not want to leave it.

From time to time memory would flash out, and an image would sear in her mind. Flooding through her suddenly, out of nowhere, the recollection would come, while she was doing something quite different. Walking upstairs, reading to the children, typing a letter.

A memory of his voice, his instruction, soft-voiced, pleasant. A memory of his hands, turning over her body, smoothing over her thighs, parting her legs, positioning her for his next round of pleasure.

Sweat would break out on her skin, nausea pool in her mouth.

She tried to fight it. Fight the flashes of memory. What had been could never be again. Sometimes, when she was very tired, the dreams were vivid in their detail. But hardest to bear, most bitter, most agonising was how that first frail illusion about Alexei had proved so cruel a lie—a lie her body had taken pleasure in… She found herself shrinking from the knowledge and increasingly shrinking from the world around her.

I have to get over it. I have to.

The words came with increasing urgency, increasing desperation, into that small, shrinking place in her mind where she now was, while the outer world faded from her, becoming more and more unreachable—even though she was moving in it, functioning, doing what she had to do, saying what she had to say. But it was is if she were living inside some kind of robot that was doing these things. Because the real her was trapped deep inside her body—the body that had betrayed her, the body that had taken pleasure in that night. And it did not matter at all that she had hurled her defiance and her fury at the man who had done it to her, telling him that she had been justified a thousand times over in taking the decision she had, to let him do that to her. In the end, she knew it did not matter.

I still feel guilty. I still feel ashamed.

That was the hard, unendurable truth she had to face.

I still feel dirty.

And I can't get clean.

Her mother worried about her, she knew, but what could she tell her?

Well, it was like this, you see. I had to keep Beaumont safe— for you, for Charlie, for all the children here—and there was only one way to do it. So I did it. And I can't undo it now. And I can't tell you what it was I did.

If she told her, she would see the disappointment in her mother's eyes. Horror. And then, worst of all, guilt that her daughter had had to do such a thing.

One of the therapists caught her one day, and suggested she was under stress.

'It's a natural reaction to all the strain you've been under, worrying about this place,' he said, sympathetically but encouragingly. 'You should take a holiday. Lots of R&R. Take it easy for a change. The clinic is fine now, and its finances are sound again—sounder than ever. You need a break, Eve.'

The man's kindness and good sense were wasted. Eve only looked at the concerned, middle-aged face and thought, *What would you think of me if you knew what I did? What would you think of me then? What would you think of me if you knew what I'd done?*

But that was something she could never say. Not to a living soul. It had to stay inside her, in that small, shrinking space inside her mind.

Taking up more and more space.

Crowding out everything. Everything else that had once been her. *Get over it! Let go of it! Ignore it!*

Hadn't 'ignore it' been the mantra that had served her all her life? The only way she'd coped with having a monster for a father, a victim for a mother? Ignoring everything she could of what her life was about—the outward wealth and glamour, the sordid travesty of family life within, where the only salvation and purpose had been to support her mother, help care for her brother and the other children at the clinic.

So why can't I ignore this?

In the small, shrinking remnant of her mind, she knew that she should seek medical help. That something had profoundly broken inside her. That the suffocating shade of depression was winding its deadly tentacles into her. But what was the point of seeking medical help? The part of her that was ill, broken, was not reachable by medical aid. And the very thought of counselling, of having some bland-faced professional sit there, hearing without a flicker of their eyes everything that she had done that night, and then, with the same dispassion in their voice as in their eyes, asking her why she felt this was a trauma, and whether her other sexual relationships had been traumatic. Did she, perhaps, feel a need to punish herself with guilt for this because it was merely the transference of guilt from some misdeed of her childhood? And, speaking of childhood, what had her relationship with her parents been like? Would she say it had been healthy and sustaining? And if not why not?

What do they know? They've heard it, but they've never felt it. Never experienced it. They can't know. They can't know.

Only I know.

And I can tell no one. No one at all.

She went for walks. Long walks through the beechwoods circling Beaumont, with the dried beech husks and leaves from the previous year crunching beneath her feet. Walking and walking, while the space she lived in shrank, atom by atom, and the world outside grew further and further away.

She didn't feel, or think, or remember. She just walked.

Mile after mile.

As if she were trying to leave something very far behind. Yet, like a ghost, it walked beside her. Inside her.

Then, one afternoon as she walked, the great beech trees arching overhead in a golden-leafed canopy against the pale blue sky, someone walked towards her.

It was a woman. Not even a woman. A girl. She was not dressed for walking through autumnal woods. She had a skirt on, not trousers, a long one that came down to her ankles. And a un-flatteringly baggy jumper with long sleeves. Her hair was short and scruffy-looking. Badly cut.

But she was pretty, Eve could see. Even the unflattering clothes could not conceal that, though the girl had made no attempt to wear make-up or look nice.

She came up to Eve.

Eve spoke first. Politely, but deliberately.

'I'm afraid this is private land,' she said. 'There is a public footpath, a right of way, but you've strayed off it. You need to go back up the slope. It's waymarked—I'm sure you'll find it.'

She smiled, if a little stiffly, waiting for the girl to turn around, reverse her steps.

She did not. She kept on coming forward. Then she halted.

'You are Eve, aren't you?' she said.

There was an accent in her voice. Eve frowned.

'I'm sorry, I don't—'

The girl lifted her hand. 'I know—you don't know me. But I know you. I know *of* you.' She took a breath, 'Please, let me talk to you. It is very important.'

Eve frowned. Who was this woman, with her strange foreign accent, her odd appearance, accosting her like this? Not a rambler, not someone who should be here.

'I'm afraid I—' she began, in her clipped voice.

The other girl shook her head. 'Please. Let me talk to you. I am sorry to do this, but I must. You see—' she took another breath '—I know Alexei.'

Eve froze. She felt it happening. Her whole body turning to ice.

She started to turn away. She had to go. Now. Fast. Run.

For her life.

More than her life.

'Don't go!' The accent was more pronounced now, as emotion shook the girl's voice. 'Don't go. Listen—*listen* to what I must tell you!'

Eve halted. Was the girl mad? Who was she? Why was she here? Why would she not go? And how did she have the temerity to mention that name?

'He's *sent* you here?' The words hissed from her.

The other girl shook her head. 'He does not know I am here. Please—*please* let me talk to you. It is about Alexei.'

A blankness descended over Eve's face.

'There is nothing I wish to hear about him. I never in all my life want to hear that name again.'

She started to turn away again. The other girl lurched forward, caught Eve's sleeve.

'Alexei saved my life. I *beg* you to listen to me!'

Slowly, Eve stilled. The other girl was very close now. Eve looked at her, her eyes frowning. There was something vaguely

familiar about her. Did she know her? Had she seen her somewhere? The girl's face teased at her.

What had she said? Alexei had saved her life? That seemed
an odd thing for him to have done. Alexei Constantin did not save
lives. He destroyed them.

She looked at the girl.

'You must be mistaken,' she said. 'That is not something
Alexei Constantin would do.'

Something flashed in the girl's eyes.

'He saved my life! And if you will *listen* to me, I will tell you
how.'

A veil came across Eve's face.

'I'm afraid I—' she began again.

'No!' The girl clutched at her sleeve again. 'Listen to me.' Eve
looked at her. The girl's eyes were burning with a fierce light. It
was strange. But then, everything was suddenly very strange. As
if something had suddenly dislocated inside her head. She should
turn and walk away, she knew. This girl, whoever she was, was
clearly disturbed. Possibly demented.

Instinctively, Eve went into a familiar role. The one her mother
had schooled her in. Putting a polite but dismissive expression on
her face, she said, 'I'm really very sorry, but I'm afraid I can't have
this conversation. I haven't the faintest idea who you are, and—'

The girl's grip on her sleeve tightened.

'My name,' she said, 'is Sofi Dimitry. For five years I was
known as Sasha. But I was always Sofi Dimitry.'

Eve tried to disengage her sleeve. The girl was staring at her with
an intense, fixed gaze. She did not loosen her grip on Eve's sleeve.

'Five years,' she said, in her hoarse, accented voice. 'Can you
imagine five years, Eve? Eighteen hundred days. Eighteen
hundred nights.'

'I'm sorry, I don't—'

'*Listen!*'

Her hand tightened on Eve's sleeve, and now, for the first time, Eve stilled. There was something in the girl's voice that chilled her blood. She was hearing her speak. Hearing the words go into her head. Hearing what the girl was telling her in her strained, accented speech. Something made her listen. The girl's eyes were fixed on her, as if willing her to hear. As if what she was saying was burning a hole through her to make its way out of her.

'My name,' she said again, 'is Sofi Dimitry. They took my name from me, but I was her all the time. All the time I was *still* Sofi Dimitry. I had to remember it—every day, every night. Every night when I was Sasha. The thing they tried to make me be. It was *hard* to remember I was Sofi Dimitry. *Hard* to remember when they were injecting me with drugs to make me easier to handle. *Hard* to remember when—' she almost stopped, her voice almost breaking '—when men were having sex with me. It was *hard*. But I *am* Sofi Dimitry. I am *not* Sasha. I am *not* that thing they made me. The thing they made me, those men who came to my village when I was sixteen, when I was Sofi Dimitry. They offered me a job. They said it would be work on a cruise ship. The tips would be very good, they said, and the ship would dock in Italy and we would be allowed in to the country to work. But it was not a cruise ship, and we did not go to Italy. We went to Istanbul. There—' her voice faltered, but she did not stop '—they put me to work. They made me Sasha. A prostitute who had to have sex with men. Many, many men. They made me Sasha,' she said again.

And now, slowly, her grip on Eve's sleeve slipped, and slowly, very slowly, she sank down to her knees on the dry-leafed ground. Her arms wrapped around her body.

'They made Sasha,' she said again. And she did not look at Eve.

But Eve looked at her. Looked at the girl who had said what could not be said but what must be said. The horror that had been done to her.

Slowly, very slowly, she knelt down beside the girl. She put her arms around the girl. It was strange. She did not know this girl. She was a stranger.

And yet not a stranger. Not a stranger at all. Someone very, very familiar. Someone who had done things—hideous things—for which she was not to blame...*not* to blame...

'You're not Sasha,' she said. 'You are Sofi Dimitry. You have always been Sofi Dimitry. They never touched you. Not the you inside. The you that you really are.'

The girl lifted her eyes to her, and suddenly they were different. Very, very different.

'And so are you, Eve. You are still who you always were. Whatever was done to you.'

The deep brown eyes held hers, and suddenly it was Eve clinging to the girl for support, because it was as if her body were suddenly boneless, as if a great weight were dragging at her. The weight of something that at last, *at last,* she could tell of. The weight of the degradation, the obscenity, the revulsion and the disgust, the shame and guilt, the anger and fury, and the burning, crushing impotence that she could not, *could not* change what had happened to her, not just on that horrible night with Alexei, but all her life, the world thinking she was her disgusting father's willing creature, as Alexei had thought her, treating her as the whore she had had *no choice* but to be. And this girl knew it. Knew all of it. Knew it a thousand, a million times worse.

And as she looked into her eyes she saw recognition there, and knew that it was in her own eyes too.

The girl spoke again, and her voice was urgent now—urgent and impelling.

'Don't you *see,* Eve? That if *I* can still be Sofi Dimitry, then you are still who you always were. Look at me, Eve, look at me! It's not our fault. Don't you *see* that? It's theirs. And if we think we are somehow to blame—' her voice broke '—then they've won. They've won. And I will *never,* never let them win.' Her expression changed. 'We have to fight, Eve. We have to fight. If we give in, we've lost. So we fight, you and I. I am not Sasha, and you—you are not what you became that night. You never were. You never will be.'

Eve looked at this girl who had spent five years in hell. Horror drenched through her again as she thought of what she had endured.

Cold went through to her very bones. She gazed into her eyes, this girl who was Sofi Dimitry, who had refused to be Sasha. Refused for five long, agonising years in hell.

'It can't touch you, Eve. Not if you don't let it. Be free of it. Be *free.*'

The weight was tearing at her, tearing her down, down.

'Let it go, Eve. Let it go.' Sofi's voice was very quiet. 'Don't look at me and say you can't. If I can do it, after five years, then you can do it.' She paused a moment, then went on speaking. 'That's why I came here. I knew when Alexei told me how you were when he tried to…to put things right. I knew it would be hard for you. I knew you would need someone who could understand.'

Eve's hands fell away. She knelt back. It was very strange, there was no weight now. Sunlight dappled through the trees. She could hear a blackbird in a tree nearby. See a squirrel scuttling along a branch. Her hands rested in her lap and she looked down at them, then back at Sofi—a girl she did not know, but who was not, despite that, a stranger.

'I know I should have told someone about what happened. Should have gone to get counselling, something. But…' Eve's voice trailed off.

The other girl gave a sad, rueful smile.

'But you were ashamed. Ashamed to say what happened to you. But I understand. And I could set you free.' She got to her feet, helping Eve up, her hand around her forearm.

As she straightened, Eve leant forward suddenly, on impulse, and reached to kiss the other girl's cheek.

'Thank you,' she said softly. Everything was different. The air was easier to breathe, the sunlight warmer, the world closer. Not far away any more.

She drew back, and as she did so she saw the girl's hand curled around her forearm.

Recognition, disbelieving and incredulous, flared through her. Despite the unflattering clothes, the bad haircut. Deliberately unflattering, deliberately bad. So that men would not look on her with lust.

Her head flew up, her eyes shocked. 'You…' she breathed. 'It was you that night. In that hotel, in the nightclub. With…'

The other nodded. 'Alexei Constantin. Yes.' She paused minutely. 'The night he saved me.'

She let her hand fall from Eve's arm.

'*Alexei?*' Eve's voice was a hiss. 'But he bought you that night. I saw him. You had just told your price—Sasha's price—to the man I was with. Then Alexei bought you, and…'

'And saved me, Eve. Yes, Alexei. You do not believe me, but it is true. Just as I did not believe that he had done what he told me he had to you—especially given your history. I did not believe it possible of him.' She took a breath. 'The Alexei you know is not the one I know. Listen to my story, because it is true.'

Every muscle in Eve's body had tensed. She didn't want to hear. Wanted to run, to cover her ears and run. But the other girl was talking, low and steady.

'When I—when *Sasha*—accosted him that night, he knew at once from my accent that I was Dalaczian, and he spoke to me in our language. He asked my price and agreed to it, and took me upstairs to his suite. And there…' Her voice became strange. 'He did not touch me. Instead—' she paused a moment, then

went on '—he talked to me. He told me he could help me if I
wanted him to. I did not believe him. Did not dare. But it was
true—all true.' She looked at Eve. 'Alexei Constantin runs an organisation that rescues women like me, either tricked or coerced
into prostitution. No one knows, because if they knew he would
become the target of very dangerous men—the men who make
money out of women like me. The men who use women like me.'

'No,' said Eve. What Sofi Dimitry said was absurd. It was
absurd. Impossible. Quite impossible. Alexei Constantin did not
do that. He did not run such an organisation. He did not rescue
girls who had been made into Sashas. 'This is not true. You are
mistaken. You are wrong. *I* am the proof that you are wrong!'
There was desperation in her voice. 'He is lying to you, trying
to trap you, do something terrible to you—to you all. Don't trust
him—*don't trust him!*'

She could hear the hysteria in her voice, but she could not
stop it. Could only feel the fear that Alexei Constantin
should somehow have succeeded in fooling this poor, deluded
creature. Of course it was not true. How could it be true? Alexei
Constantin was every bit as foul as her father.

But the other girl only shook her head.

She got to her feet, holding out her hand to Eve.

'Come,' she said. 'Come and see.'

It was the house Eve had bought to rehouse the clinic. Alexei
must have kept it for himself, she realised.

She wasn't sure how many girls were there. Some spoke
English well; some did not. Some were Dalaczian, some from
other Eastern European countries.

'For some,' said Sofi quietly, 'only their bodies have been
rescued. Some still live with the demons they endured. They feel
they can never be clean. Even though the fault is not theirs, but
that of the men who did this to them, who bought them and used

them.' Her expression changed. Became bitter. 'It is strange…had we been prisoners of war, suffered physical abuse and violence, even torture, we would be regarded as heroines. But because we were worked as prostitutes we are treated with contempt, even though we did not wish to do those things.'

Eve looked about her. At the girls and women whose lives had been usurped and destroyed, and who would still be outcasts, looked down on for what had been done to them. How many could return home, have husbands, children, now?

'You are all heroines,' she said in a low, troubled voice. 'Each and every one of you.' She drew a little way away. 'Why did you help me, Sofi?'

The other girl gave a sad smile.

'For your sake, and for Alexei's.'

Eve halted. 'Sofi—how—*how* could he do to me what he did, when he does—' she indicated with a sweep of her hand '—all this? *How?*'

A troubled expression crossed Sofi's face.

'He told me he tried to explain to you, but you were too angry.'

Eve's face stiffened. 'How can there *possibly* be an explanation?'

Sofi shook her head. 'Eve, it is hard. But this is not something for you to ask me. You must ask him.'

'I'm not going near him again.'

'Eve, you must. You must. Give him a chance—one chance. That is all.'

There was pain in her voice, and Eve looked at her. Through her own distress she could hear the other girl's as well. Slowly, she spoke.

'You're in love with him, aren't you?'

Sofi looked away, then back. 'It was—what is the word that psychologists use?—transference. He rescued me, so I fell in love with him a little. But now I don't need that any more. Now he is only a friend—a friend who turned to me because I could see…he needed help. So he told me, Eve. He told me why, and he told me of the guilt that tears him apart for what he did to you.' Her voice dropped. 'Do it for me, Eve, and for the others here. Alexei does so much for us, for so many like us.'

Emotion worked in Eve's face. It hurt. It hurt badly.

'I can't!'

'One chance, Eve, that's all I ask you give him. Please.' She paused. 'He's in his offices in London. I will tell him you are coming. You can go to him now—now that you are free of your burden. But there is another freedom you need, Eve, and only Alexei can give you that. Only Alexei. So, please, go to him.'

Slowly, very slowly, with emotion roiling in her—emotion she could make no sense of, conflicting and confusing—Eve turned, and left.

CHAPTER ELEVEN

THE TRAIN ate up the miles into London. She had not been there since she had fled from Alexei. Now she had to face him again. Dread pooled in her stomach and her hands clenched in her lap. And yet it was more than dread.

But what she did not know.

Did not dare ask.

The office, into which she had been ushered without being asked why she wanted to see Alexei Constantin—he was, she presumed, expecting her to turn up—was still the same. The moss-green carpet, the deep green velvet curtains, the panelled walls with their landscaped paintings, the grate with its flowers—autumnal now, not those of late spring.

And the man at the desk was still the same. Eve felt her breath tighten in her lungs, felt her heart start to hammer in her chest. God, she should not have come. She should never have come.

But she stood her ground, digging her heels into the carpet, willing herself not to move, to stand still. Emotion seethed and surged within her like a restless tide. She clenched her jaw. She *must* do this.

Through the veil of tension lacing her, she watched him get to his feet. His movements were jerky, she registered. But it was his face that sent a ripple of shock through her. It was gaunt and grey, as if he did not eat, did not sleep.

And yet it was more than shock that went through her as she watched him come towards her. It was something familiar, something she must not allow.

Words burst from her, wild and uncontrolled. Straight to the heart of what she *had* to know. What made no sense.

'Why did you do it? Why did you do it to me? It doesn't make sense! You rescue girls like Sofi, and then treat me like that. It doesn't make sense.'

Her voice was staccato, abrupt. Hostile.

He stopped. The greyness in his face seemed to increase.

'I tried to tell you. It was because I thought…I thought you were like your father.'

His voice was low and strained, and he stood very, very still. His eyes seemed to want to search her face, and yet he stopped them doing so. As if he had no right.

She could feel her throat choking.

'You didn't have any right to find that out the way you did!'

'I know,' he said, in that low voice. 'I've known that from when I…' He paused, then visibly forced himself to continue. 'When I discovered the truth of what had…motivated…your behaviour. It crucified me, Eve, finding out why you—why you…' His voice cut off, unable to finish.

His face was stark and drawn, and he looked twenty years older suddenly.

'It crucified me.'

His voice shook, and suddenly, like pincers in her lungs, Eve felt something go through her that was impossible. Impossible to feel about Alexei Constantin. Quite impossible.

Because the man was a monster—a monster who had blackmailed her for her body, deliberately and callously, thinking she deserved nothing better.

So how could she be standing here—with emotion racing

through her, after everything she had been through at the hands of this man—be standing here feeling pity for him?

And yet she did. Because there was something about the way he was standing there, saying those agonising words—something that pierced through the angry, tumult in her breast.

I can't feel pity for him. It's insane.

She was fighting it, she knew. Fighting hard, very hard, against something that was inside her now. Deep inside. But trying to come out.

He was speaking again, the words coming as if he could not bear to say them, as if they were unsayable. And yet he was making himself say them.

'It crucified me because as I stood watching your brother, watching the other children and realising just what it was that I had done, I knew that I had become the person I had spent my life hunting down so that I could destroy him. I had become him. And all those like him. Now I was one of them.'

He looked at her. His gaze was coming as if from very far away. A cold, arctic place, where lost souls wandered in eternity.

'I had become a man like your father. The man—' He seemed to have difficulty speaking, the words being forced from him. 'The man I've spent my life hunting down. Seeking to destroy.'

The air was pressing around her, pressing in from the sides of the room, thick and heavy.

She stood, her whole body clenched, looking at him where he stood, ramrod-straight, but with such tension coming from him that it seemed to shimmer in the air, to crackle like an electric storm.

'Why?' Her voice was a whisper. 'Why? What did he do to you?'

His dark eyes rested on her. Seeing her, but not seeing her. Seeing someone else.

Slowly, haltingly, the words grated from him.

'When I was a child, my parents were killed in an earthquake.

There was no one left in my family. Only…' He paused, almost unable to continue. 'Only my sister. Ileana. She looked after me. She was all I had. Then, when I was ten, she went away. She took a job. A job that would pay enough money to keep me at school. It was a very good school, and there were very few of them then in Dalaczia. It was run by monks, and it was a boarding school. Ileana knew, as our parents had known, that if I could stay at school there it would give me the chance to break out of the life that most village boys were fated for. It would give me the education to get to university, to have a profession, a better life. But when our parents died there was no money. The country was in chaos, both from the earthquake and from the political upheaval all around in that part of the world. There was no hope—none. Not for anyone. Only Ileana could pay for my education, and only if she went to work abroad.'

He paused again. Eve stood very still. Cold had started to pool in her stomach.

Slowly he started to speak again, his eyes resting on her.

'Do I need to tell you what the work abroad was? You've met Sofi. You've met the other women who did such work. That is what happened to Ileana. Do I know if she knew beforehand what it was that she would have to do? I cannot tell. I still, after all these years, cannot tell. But I think she did know. There was a sorrow in her eyes when she said goodbye to me that was more than sorrow at parting from me. I think she knew exactly what she was going to have to do to look after me, to give me the future that our parents had wanted for me. And that is why—' He stopped. As if the words had simply cut out.

A long, terrible shudder went through him.

'And that is why, that day—oh, God, Eve—that day when you looked at me, said to me, "Come and see—"'

Again his voice cut out, his throat working.

'When I saw the children in their wheelchairs, when I saw your brother…'

He looked at her. The expression in his eyes was unbearable. The claws in her lungs clutched at her breath, crushing it from her.

'You were Ileana. The sister who sacrificed herself for her brother. And I—' Revulsion twisted in his voice. 'I had become a man like your father—like all those men who do such things as were done to my sister, to Sofi, to all those women.'

He fell silent. The silence stretched like a long, long skein of time, reaching back into the past, reaching out into the present. The present where Eve stood. She could feel the blood stilling in her veins as she asked the question she knew she had to ask, but which hung like a dread over her.

'Where is Ileana? Where is she now, Alexei?'

He didn't speak. Just stood looking at her. Eve waited, knowing the final blow was yet to fall.

And then it fell.

'Your father killed her. He gave a party in a beach house owned by a government minister in some corrupt African state. He invited special guests, for special entertainment. But one of the girls annoyed him. Refused to perform the act he wanted of her. It required specialist…equipment…and she refused. So he beat her. He beat her to death.'

Time had stopped. Swallowed up in horror. Sickness poured through Eve.

'My father killed your sister.'

Her voice was blank, empty of all but horror. All but sickness. From a long, long distance she could hear Alexei still talking. He seemed to be fading in and out.

'It took me a long time to uncover the truth of how she died— that she had died at all. For there was no inquest, of course. Your father was a wealthy, powerful man even then, and the minister in question was currying favour with this rich European who had, so it happened, a bad temper… And of course the girl who'd died was no one—no one at all. A whore. Who would miss her? No one. Whores have no family, no friends. Only the men who pimp them and the men who use them for sex. But Ileana *did* have friends—friends who had been there, seen her die. And though it took me years to trace and track them, I found those who were prepared to overcome their fear and tell me what had happened that night. They did not dare testify—and even if they had, would your father ever have faced trial in a country where the rich and powerful dispose of those who trouble them without let or hindrance by the law? So I knew.' There was the minutest pause, and then continuance. 'I knew I had to exact justice in my own way.'

There was silence again.

'I did not have to kill him. I merely had to deliver him to those who would do so. Who would be the executioners of my sister's murderer.'

He looked at Eve.

'He did not die an easy death, your father.' The words came from him without emotion. 'It takes time to beat a man to death.'

She heard the words. Heard them fall in her head like stones.

Justice. Her father had received justice.

For all his crimes.

So many crimes.

And the very worst crime of all…murder. Murder…

She felt the air thicken around her, a black mist swirling up to her. Felt the room tilt about her.

And then arms—strong, unyielding arms—that lowered her carefully, gently, onto a chair. Her head bowed, then straightened, her eyes regained vision.

Immediately, as if she were red hot, he released her. She swayed again, then recovered.

'Oh, God, Eve, I'm sorry. I'm sorry. I should not have told you. I should never have told you!'

She shook her head negatingly.

'No,' she said. 'No…'

Slowly, she rubbed a hand across her brow. Alexei stood back, outlined against the light from the window. A dark shape against the light.

'How much you must have hated me.' Her voice was low, subdued. 'For being his daughter.'

'Hated you?'

His voice was strange.

'How could you not?' she said heavily.

She started to get up. There was no point staying here. None. The horror that she had heard made it impossible. So much horror.

So much hatred.

Too much to bear.

Too much to overcome. Nothing could overcome such hatred. Such horror.

The room swirled around her as she tried to stand, and she sank back again. Wave upon wave was going through her body.

'Eve!'

She moved her head and her vision cleared blearily. Alexei's hands were on her elbows to steady her, and then, as before, he dropped his hands away. As if she were red-hot.

Or diseased. Contaminated.

Contaminated by her father's blood in her. The father who had had his sister's blood on his hands.

She looked at him bleakly. 'You did what you did to me to punish me. To punish me for being his daughter. I understand that now.'

He bowed his head in bitter acknowledgement.

'And now I am punished in my turn.' His voice was harsh, like an arctic wind blowing. 'Punished by your hatred of me. My hatred of myself. Of what I have become. A man like your father.'

Slowly, painfully, she shook her head. 'You cannot say that. You cannot say you are like a man who uses prostitutes, who kills them.'

'That is not why I am like your father, Eve. I am like your father because—' He took a razored breath. 'Because I took pleasure in the sex that I had with you. I found it erotic, exciting. I found it arousing.' He looked at her, and in his eyes she could see something that terrified her, that same blankness, as if all humanity had absented itself from him. 'I could not have done what I did to you, Eve, if I had not found it arousing.'

His eyes bored down at her.

'Like you said, Eve, I *made* you spend the night with me. And though afterwards what I had done revolted me, yet at the time I still enjoyed it. And *that* is why I am like men like your father.'

Suddenly she was on her feet.

'But you're *not!* God Almighty, do you think men like my father think they are scum? Of course they don't. They think the girls they use are scum, but not themselves. Oh, no, *they* are upright citizens of the world. Captains of industry, professional men, respectable men, husbands and fathers. They can't *possibly* be like the whores and the tarts they use and abuse.' She took a step forward, her eyes blazing. 'But *you* know different. You know what you did, and hated yourself for it. Hated that you had succumbed to the lures of the woman you thought me! And that means you are *not* like them. You are *not!*'

Something was happening to his eyes. That terrifying blankness was shifting.

'Eve, I don't deserve your forgiveness. Don't absolve me for what I did to you. I don't deserve it.'

Her eyes held his. Held them even against the great weight that was dragging at him, dragging him down, making it hard, so hard, to hold him. But she held him. Her eyes held him.

'But you can let go. You can let go of what you did. Let go, Alexei. You are a good man. And you have suffered much. Allow yourself…' She took a deep, shuddering breath as her eyes still held his, held him, as the weight dragging him down seemed to shift, to loosen. 'Allow yourself to let go of this *one* crime you committed.' She paused. Something was lightening inside her too, something that made the holding of his eyes no burden—no burden at all.

'Alexei—the Egyptians believed that their souls would be weighed against a feather, and I tell you now that yours would soar, *soar* into the heavens! Think of all the good you've done— are still doing. Think of the girls you've rescued, and are still rescuing. You meted out justice to a murderer, a monster who killed your sister, who used his fists on my defenceless mother, who crippled his own son. Without you, my father would still be free to hurt and maim, possibly even to kill again. He had to be stopped, and you stopped him. And so, yes, I *do* absolve you. I absolve you absolutely, entirely. And now—' her throat tightened '—now you must absolve yourself. You *must,* Alexei.'

She moved towards him. He stood stiff and still, so very still. But in his eyes, something was moving, showing.

'Alexei—listen to me. Both our lives have been blighted and cursed by my father. He caused so much horror, so much hatred. We *can't* let him win now.' She took another breath. 'Sofi said to me that we *have* to fight, and she is right. We *do* have to fight. We can't give in. We can't give in to the hatred, the horror. The corruption. So let us fight it. Together, Alexei. We will fight it together.'

She reached towards him. Her hand moving to his face. He did not move. His face was a mask, a mask drawn tight over him. Only in his eyes was there anything, anything at all.

She laid her hand against his cheek and felt a tremor go through him, very deep. Her heart swelled, emotion filling it.

'We can do this, Alexei. We can fight, and we can win,' she said softly. She drew closer, her other hand reaching to smooth with infinite care the feathering of hair at his brow. She felt the tremor come again, and still she held his eyes—held him. 'And this is how we fight. Like this.'

She lifted her face to his, and softly, so very softly, touched her mouth to his.

'Like this,' she whispered, and her eyes were glowing—glowing with a power that was stronger than hatred, stronger than horror, stronger than corruption.

'Make love to me, Alexei. Make love to me. Use the gift of sex for its true purpose. Not to corrupt, but to celebrate. To celebrate our humanity. And even more—more than our humanity.'

She let her hands fall slowly down.

'We had one moment, Alexei. One moment, you and I, when we saw each other as we really are. For those few brief, precious moments we stood by the edge of the sea in the moonlight and saw each other as we really are. Our true selves. And then both of us afterwards thought it was nothing more than an illusion, a fantasy of our own making. But the illusion was the truth. The fantasy was the reality.'

His voice cracked. 'I was trying to find that again. Oh, dear God, Eve, believe that if you believe nothing else. Believe that all I hoped for when I put you to that nightmare test was that I would find again the woman I had found that night. The woman I had followed, would follow again—into the mouth of hell, if that was where she went. *That's* who I so desperately wanted to find again. To find her real, alive—the true woman I so desperately wanted you to be. The woman…' He took a long, shuddering breath. 'The woman I wanted to fall in love with.'

His face etched with pain again. He hadn't seen how light had leapt in her eyes as he spoke, had seen only his own inner darkness.

'And when I did not find her—when all found was what I thought was the corrupt creature of the man I hated with all my power—then…' His voice dropped. 'Then I wanted to punish you for being that creature. For destroying my hope. My desperate hope that the fantasy I had kissed in the moonlight, with the starlight in her hair, was real.'

Softness was in her face.

'But she *is* real. I *am* that reality you sought. And the fact that you sought it—oh, Alexei—that you tried to find me, the *real* me, after I'd fled from you because all the weight of my past, my present, was crushing me down, making it impossible to hope that anyone could rescue me from the life I was trapped in, could rescue me with love, *that* shows to me that you are the reality I sought.'

She held her hands out to him, as if beseechingly. The light streamed from her eyes—a light to light their way.

'Be my reality,' she said. 'And be—' Her voice cracked. 'Be the man I love. Oh, please be that, Alexei! Because I need you. I need you so very, very much…'

The tears spilled from her eyes, and as they did, with a cry, he started forward, wrapping her in his arms, enfolding her.

'Eve! Oh, God, Eve!'

Words poured from him. She did not understand them, but it did not matter. She knew what they spoke of, and as her head bowed against the strong wall of his chest, her weeping deepened. He held her, strong and sheltering, while she wept. And while her face was still wet with tears he lifted it between his hands and gazed down into her eyes. And what she saw there was like a bright light shining. Banishing the dark.

'*My only love, sprung from my only hate.*' His eyes blazed down at her. 'My own miracle. The greatest gift I could ever receive. Your love—'

She looked up at him, her fingers entwining with his.

'And I have yours. I see it in your eyes.'

'And your eyes,' he said, as his mouth lowered to hers, 'will never weep again. Because I give my life to you—my life and my love, for all my days.'

'For all *our* days,' she said. 'But I *will* weep, Alexei. I will weep again. Because at last—after so long, so many years of having always to hide everything I felt, show no emotion because it was too dangerous, too agonising—at last I can show my feelings. I never cried, never allowed myself to cry, and now I *can* cry. And I will again. But you'll be happy for me then, I promise you. I *promise* you.' She kissed him softly. 'Trust me, they will be happy tears.'

EPILOGUE

IN THE dim light, two bodies moved. Moonlight played on pale bare limbs, catching the rich swathe of golden hair, the dark sable head lowering to kiss the upturned face that lay on the pillow.

'My adored, beautiful Eve.' Alexei's voice was warm and loving.

Eve ran her hand down the long, sculpted length of his spine, glorying in the strength and smoothness of his muscled back. Wonder filled her. Wonder and gratitude and so much love. Love had washed away the last traces of hatred and horror, of the torment and the doubt that had divided them so bitterly, so terrifyingly.

She felt tears prick in her eyes again.

Alexei saw them, his expression changing.

'Eve, no, don't cry. Please don't cry!'

She smiled through the tears, coming, as they did now, so often.

'It's because I'm happy,' she said. 'Happy for the first time in my life. And at peace. *You* are my peace, Alexei.'

Her hand glided to smooth his hair, shaping his skull as he lay over her, their bodies fast entwined.

He kissed her eyes, one and then the other, tasting her tears.

'No more tears. Not now,' he murmured, his hand cradling her face, his thumb gently, so gently, brushing the diamond drops away.

And for the space of time that it took for their bodies to fuse, and merge, and melt into the joyous incandescence that was the perfect physical expression of their feelings for each other, a union not just of their bodies but of their hearts, she did not weep.

But as the ecstasy ebbed gently from her and she lay in his arms complete, perfected, she cradled him against her, holding him close, she felt tears come again.

He let her weep, rocking her and soothing her, murmuring to her words in his own language of love and cherishing. And as, at last, she stilled, he spoke.

'You are my love and my beloved. My adored, beautiful Eve. Will you marry me and be my wife? Will you let me worship you with my body, with my soul, and love you will all my being? With all my heart?'

She gazed at him, her heart full.

'Yes,' she said. 'Oh, yes. With all my heart.'

And she held him closer yet.

She wept on her wedding day—and so did her mother, and many others. Charlie and his friends, however, stared, bemused, at the strange things adults did, even when they were supposed to be happy. But he gave his sister away all the same, gliding his wheelchair expertly along beside her in her white satin and lace as she walked slowly up the aisle to the swell of the organ in the parish church. And he grinned with an encouraging thumbs-up at Alexei, who seemed to have a strange, dopey expression on his face as he took his bride's hand at the altar rail—which was odd, because he was usually a cool guy, and Charlie was glad he was going to marry Evie and live at Beaumont with them. Then having done his duty, he executed a neat donut reverse, and backed his wheelchair next to his mother, who seemed to be crying as well. It seemed nuts to Charlie—but then, that was grown-ups for you. They were weird.

He settled back to watch the wedding.

At the altar rail, Alexei gazed at Eve. She was blindingly beautiful, like a bright, shining jewel, a rare and precious pearl, and his breath caught in his throat.

'I am so blessed,' he said softly, as the vicar came towards them to begin the service. 'So very, very blessed.'

He caught her hand and lifted it reverently, lovingly to his lips.

Eve felt her heart soar with happiness. A happiness that would never, *could* never end. Because she was with the man she loved.

And tears, like diamonds, started in her eyes.

Alexei saw them.

'Happy tears,' she told him. 'Happy tears.'

UNCUT

Even more passion for your reading pleasure!

Escape into a world of intense passion and scorching
romance! Everything you've always loved in
Harlequin Presents books, but we've turned up
the thermostat just a little, so that the relationships
really sizzle....

Kimberley's little boy is in danger, and the only person
who can help is his father. But Luc doesn't even know
his son exists. The gorgeous Brazilian tycoon will help—
provided Kimberley sleeps with him....

MILLION-DOLLAR LOVE-CHILD

by Sarah Morgan

Available November 2006.
Don't miss it!

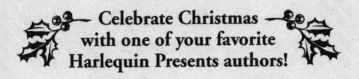
THE SICILIAN'S CHRISTMAS BRIDE

by **Sandra Marton**

On sale November 2006.

When Maya Sommers becomes Dante Russo's
mistress, rules are made. Although their affair
will be highly satisfying in the bedroom,
there'll be no commitment or future plans.
Then Maya discovers she's pregnant....

Get your copy today!

If you enjoyed what you just read,
then we've got an offer you can't resist!

Take 2 bestselling
love stories FREE!

Plus get a FREE surprise gift!

Clip this page and mail it to Harlequin Reader Service®

IN U.S.A.	IN CANADA
3010 Walden Ave.	P.O. Box 609
P.O. Box 1867	Fort Erie, Ontario
Buffalo, N.Y. 14240-1867	L2A 5X3

YES! Please send me 2 free Harlequin Presents® novels and my free surprise gift. After receiving them, if I don't wish to receive anymore, I can return the shipping statement marked cancel. If I don't cancel, I will receive 6 brand-new novels every month, before they're available in stores! In the U.S.A., bill me at the bargain price of $3.80 plus 25¢ shipping & handling per book and applicable sales tax, if any*. In Canada, bill me at the bargain price of $4.47 plus 25¢ shipping & handling per book and applicable taxes**. That's the complete price and a savings of at least 10% off the cover prices—what a great deal! I understand that accepting the 2 free books and gift places me under no obligation ever to buy any books. I can always return a shipment and cancel at any time. Even if I never buy another book from Harlequin, the 2 free books and gift are mine to keep forever.

106 HDN DZ7Y
306 HDN DZ7Z

Name	(PLEASE PRINT)	
Address	Apt.#	
City	State/Prov.	Zip/Postal Code

Not valid to current Harlequin Presents® subscribers.

Want to try two free books from another series?
Call 1-800-873-8635 or visit www.morefreebooks.com.

* Terms and prices subject to change without notice. Sales tax applicable in N.Y.
** Canadian residents will be charged applicable provincial taxes and GST.
   All orders subject to approval. Offer limited to one per household.
   ® are registered trademarks owned and used by the trademark owner and or its licensee.

PRES04R   ©2004 Harlequin Enterprises Limited

*They're the men who have
everything—except brides...*

Wealth, power, charm—what else could a heart-stoppingly
handsome tycoon need? In the GREEK TYCOONS miniseries
you have already been introduced to some gorgeous
Greek multimillionaires who are in need of wives.

Now it's the turn of favorite Presents author

Lynne Graham,

with her attention-grabbing romance...

RELUCTANT MISTRESS, BLACKMAILED WIFE

On sale November 2006.

This tycoon has met his match, and he's decided
he has to have her...whatever it takes!